The Willow Man

Sue Purkiss is the author of several novels for young readers including *Spook School*, *Changing Brooms* and *Spooks Away*, which are about ghosts, witches and ghosts again.

"I came to write *The Willow Man*," she says, "after becoming fascinated by the figure of the Willow Man itself, which you see when you drive past Bridgwater down the M5 motorway. It all came together – the experience of working with troubled young people and of my daughter having a stroke when she was seven. I suddenly saw the Willow Man as symbolizing the physical, mental and emotional barriers which can sometimes get in the way of young people living their lives as they should be able to live them."

Sue lives in Cheddar, Somerset, and spends her time writing and working as a teacher for a youth offending team.

D1627986

The Willow Man

Sue Purkiss

WALKER BOOKS
AND SUBSIDIARIES
LONDON · BOSTON · SYDNEY · AUCKLAND

Serena de la Hey created the original Willow Man, which stands beside the M5 in Somerset. My thanks to her, both for making it in the first place and for giving me the time to show me how she wove living willow into a sculpture.

First published 2006 by Walker Books Ltd
87 Vauxhall Walk, London SE11 5HJ

2 4 6 8 10 9 7 5 3 1

Text © 2006 Sue Purkiss
Cover illustration © 2006 Phil Schramm

The right of Sue Purkiss to be identified as author of this work has been asserted by her in accordance with the Copyright, Designs and Patents Act 1988

This book has been typeset in Sabon

Printed and bound in Great Britain by Bookmarque Ltd, Croydon, Surrey

British Library Cataloguing in Publication Data:
a catalogue record for this book is available
from the British Library

ISBN-13: 978-1-84428-115-2
ISBN-10: 1-84428-115-9

www.walkerbooks.co.uk

Contents

For Katie, Tim and Richard.
And for children anywhere who
feel that no one is listening.

Bad Things Happen

He was forty feet tall. His arms extended proudly, like an actor gracefully accepting applause – "Look at me! Praise me! Worship me!" His powerful torso was twisted at a slight angle to his massive thighs, so that his small head gazed with a mixture of defiance and contempt across the concrete ribbon of the motorway. He seemed to be perfectly balanced on one leg: the other was bent, as if at any moment he might choose to complete the step and take his freedom.

He was the Willow Man. Some called him an angel, the Angel of the South. He was both young and old. Within him, woven with the living willow into his great frame, power lay coiled. But the power was captive. Strong as he was, he could not move.

Tom Healey liked the Willow Man. Every time they drove back from the hospital down the motorway, he would twist round to gaze at the huge dark figure for as long as possible. He could see it from his bedroom window as well, but only as a small figure across the fields. Tom felt that it would be no surprise if one day those powerful thighs began to move. The giant would cross the road in two strides, crushing cars and lorries as it went. It wouldn't stop to look down; it wouldn't even notice. People would die, lives would be changed forever, but the Willow Man wouldn't care. It would just disappear into the distance, full of its own mysterious purpose, leaving chaos behind it. Because bad things happen like that. Tom knew this now.

Sometimes he talked to Sophie about the Willow Man. They had both seen the huge scaffold which was used to construct the metal framework of the figure, but the willow skin had been woven since Sophie went into hospital. She'd been fascinated by the early stages of the giant, and she seemed to be listening when Tom told her about how it was growing. It was difficult to find things he could talk to her about. She didn't seem interested in anything much, not now.

Sophie was Tom's sister. She was eight, four years younger than him. She had been in hospital for a while now. The hospital was miles away, on the other side of Bristol, but she had to be there because of what was wrong with her. Tom's mother was there too, helping to look after her. Tom and his dad went up once a week to see them, or sometimes Dad went by himself straight from school. Tom didn't much like going to the hospital. There was a lot he didn't like about the way life was at the moment, the way it had been since Sophie had her stroke. He knew it was selfish to feel that way though, so he didn't mention it to anyone.

Sophie became ill one morning at breakfast. There was no warning. One minute life was normal; the next it wasn't. Sophie and Tom had been arguing about juice. Sophie said Tom had taken too much and not left her any, and he ought to have given her some from his glass. Tom said there wasn't enough for both of them. Sophie said he was a selfish pig, *and* he'd finished off the honey nut loops, and she *was* going to have some of his juice. She'd grabbed the glass, he'd grabbed it back, the orange juice had splattered all over the table, and Mum had erupted.

"Oh, for heaven's sake! Sophie, behave! Look what you've done! And we're late already. Get the cloth and wipe it up – come on."

Sophie's mouth had started to tremble. "You always blame me for everything and it's not fair. It was—"

"Now, there's no need to start crying – Sophie?

Sophie? What's the matter...?"

Sophie had gone very pale. She'd put her hands to her head, and she'd been a bit sick, and then she'd gone all wobbly, and Mum had called the doctor, and he'd said he didn't know what was wrong, and he thought they'd better go up to the children's hospital. And now she couldn't walk or talk, and when she smiled, the smile was on only one side of her face. It was because she was paralyzed on her right side. Her left side was fine, but nothing on the right worked any more. They said it was a stroke, and it only ever happened to one child in fifty thousand, and it was just really bad luck for Sophie that it had happened to her.

That's what the doctors *said*, and most of the time Tom believed them. But just occasionally he wondered if it would still have happened if they hadn't been arguing.

Or if he hadn't taken all the juice in the first place – or if he hadn't finished off the honey nut loops...

All the same, there *hadn't* been enough juice for both of them. There really hadn't.

It wasn't something he'd talked about to anyone. Dad was either busy or tired or both, and Mum was up at the hospital all the time. It was a bit of a worry.

At first it was just Dad who went to visit. But after

a few days, Dad asked Tom if he'd like to go too. Part of him – quite a lot of him, actually – really wanted to say no. He'd never been to a hospital before and he felt nervous of what he might see.

And then there was Sophie herself. What was she going to be like? This was a serious, scary thing that had happened to her. It made the grown-ups talk in hushed tones. If you looked into their eyes, you could see that they felt frightened and helpless, that they didn't know what to say. So how was *he* supposed to know how to handle it?

Still, he knew he needed to see her. It would be better to know what she was like now than just to imagine. And anyway, he wanted to see Mum.

Sophie was still in the children's hospital then. It was quite exciting going into Bristol, seeing the suspension bridge and the boats along the water-front. The hospital was an old building on a steep hill. Inside there were impressive signs all over the place saying dramatic things like "Accident and Emergency" and "Cardiology Department" – but there wasn't much time to look, because Dad obviously knew the way and walked quickly along the brightly lit corridors.

The ward was long and narrow, and seemed full of people. Two little boys came running up and almost crashed into them; they were Batman and Robin, in cloaks and masks. They didn't seem very ill. Perhaps they'd just dropped in for a visit.

Tom followed Dad towards the far end of the ward. Facing them was a bed with high sides and lots of pillows. At first he thought it might be Sophie's, but then he realized it couldn't be because whoever was in it, lying very still under the white covers, was much too small to be Sophie. Also, there were large stuffed toys around the bed and framed photographs on the cupboard beside it; this person – this very small person – seemed to be well settled in. There was a man sitting beside the bed. As Tom watched, he put down the newspaper he'd been reading and leaned over towards the child in the bed, touching her face and then straightening the covers and smoothing them gently. He saw Tom watching and smiled at him. Tom smiled back, but he felt a bit guilty. He hoped the man wouldn't think he was being nosey.

His father stopped beside a bed on the right, and Tom saw Mum. She looked pale and strained, and her hair was all anyhow. She hugged Tom and asked if he was all right, but he could tell she wasn't really expecting a reply. Her eyes kept straying towards the bed, where Sophie was.

Sophie was asleep. Her right arm was resting on a pillow, like a crown on a cushion in a storybook. Her wavy blonde hair was matted and dull. There was a tall metal contraption beside the bed with a bag of transparent liquid at the top, which had a tube coming out of it. The other end of the tube seemed to be going into her left hand.

"What's that for?" asked Tom.

"They don't know yet if she can swallow properly, so that's just to make sure she's getting all the liquid she needs," said Mum. Her eyes were on Sophie all the time.

Tom was silent for a moment, taking it in.

"And why's her hair like that?" Sophie took a lot of care with her hair. She was always doing things with it: putting it up or trying to make it go into plaits when it wasn't really quite long enough. She would hate for it to look all scruffy.

"Well, she was sick the night she came in. It was while she was lying on a stretcher, so it all went in her hair. And then this morning she had some sort of brain scan – they stuck electrodes on her hair. I mean, really stuck them, with glue. That was horrible. She cried when they took them off. It's the only time she's cried."

Mum looked for a very bad moment as if she was going to cry too, so Tom said hastily, "Can't they wash it?"

"Yes, they're going to. But I don't quite know how. She can't sit up or anything, you see."

"Oh." Tom couldn't think of anything else to say, but Dad came to the rescue.

"Look," he said, rummaging in the bag he'd brought, "loads of people have sent cards. The news seems to have got round very quickly. Everyone's been very kind."

Sophie stirred and her eyes opened. Mum tried to show her the cards, pointing at the pictures and reading the messages. The old Sophie would have loved all the attention, but the new one didn't seem to care. She glanced at the first one or two and then turned her head away listlessly.

He found out later why her right arm, the one that didn't work now, had to be propped up. If it wasn't, it would just flop down helplessly beside the bed. Sophie had no control over it – it was as if it didn't belong to her. Over the next few days and weeks, everyone kept saying she mustn't forget about it; she had to remember it was there and try to make it work again. Their words didn't seem to have much impact on Sophie; you could tell she wasn't bothering to listen.

The oddest thing was that she couldn't talk. Sophie, who could talk for Britain, had no words. Not a single one. Sophie was silenced.

As the days went on, they realized that it wasn't just that she wasn't able to walk or talk or use her arm. It was as if a screen had come down between her and the world, and the old Sophie was locked away somewhere far, far behind it. The old Sophie would have been thrilled with the cards and the presents people had sent. The new Sophie wasn't interested. Except in one thing. Mum had bought her a huge, floppy toy dog, a St Bernard, soft and velvety. She liked him. She held him in the curve of her left arm and kept him perfectly safe.

After about a week, when the doctors had done enough tests to be absolutely sure that it was a stroke and not something else – at one stage they thought it might be some rare disease with a funny name that no one had ever heard of – they moved her to Frenchay Hospital. It was further from home, but it specialized in illnesses to do with the brain and the nervous system, and they'd be able to look after her better there. The buildings were old, but they'd decorated the children's ward with pastel-coloured paint and murals of cartoon characters, so it was bright and cheerful. But it had a funny, persistent smell, like boiled cabbage. And some of the patients worried him. There was one who never got out of bed. She couldn't even feed herself, and sometimes she groaned. He was thankful that Sophie didn't groan.

But there were some good things about the hospital. There was a schoolroom and two teachers who came in each morning, but the children could choose not to do schoolwork if they didn't feel like it. And they each had a television beside the bed, so they could sit and watch videos whenever they wanted. There were loads to choose from. Tom felt quite jealous about that.

He was always relieved to be going home. But home was odd too. People came and went and brought presents and made meals and asked about Sophie, and his grandmother came and stayed for a few days, but it wasn't the same as having Mum there. He watched television a lot too. He didn't really need to bother with homework. No one would mind if he didn't do it. The teachers at school knew what had happened to Sophie, and they stepped carefully round him. And Dad was so busy, what with going to hospital and talking on the phone to people about how Sophie was getting on, that he didn't really notice what Tom was or wasn't doing.

Once, after they'd got back from the hospital, Tom had looked out of his window at the Willow Man, small in the distance. There was a full moon, and the dark figure was sharply outlined against the cold, silver light. It looked restless, poised ready to run.

"Perhaps you will one day," whispered Tom. "Perhaps one day, you'll just find that you can. And then you'll go. You'll just pick up your feet, one after the other, and go."

Like the Wind

One night when they arrived at the hospital, Sophie was asleep and a nurse was checking her blood pressure. Tom felt anxious. He hadn't seen them doing that before. Had something happened? But Mum looked OK. She was sitting beside the bed in an armchair, idly turning the pages of a magazine. She smiled when she saw them. Tom felt relieved. It was a pretty feeble smile, but still, it was better than nothing. She wouldn't have smiled if Sophie was worse.

"Sophie had an angiogram this morning," she told them.

"A whatogram?" asked Tom.

"An angiogram. It means they gave her a general anaesthetic – that's why she's so sleepy, and why they have to keep checking her blood pressure. Then they injected a sort of dye into her blood to make the veins and arteries show up when they did a scan. It's to help them find out what damage the stroke did."

"But they know that already, don't they?" said Tom, puzzled. "I mean, they know that she can't use her right side any more."

"Yes," said Dad, "but they might have to do an operation to make sure that – oh, I don't know. But they might."

"What sort of an operation?"

"Well – on her brain."

Mum put her hand up to her mouth, making a funny little sound, and hurried off. Dad looked after her and then back at Tom. Then he turned and looked at Sophie. When she was asleep, she looked like the old Sophie. Her hair was gleaming and shiny again. Her eyelashes lay long and dark on the curve of her cheek.

After a bit, Mum came back carrying cups of tea. Her eyes were red again. Tom couldn't ever remember seeing her cry before the stroke had happened, but he knew she was crying a lot now, even though she always scurried off to try and hide the signs. "I've been thinking," she said carefully. "If she does need to have an operation, they'll have to cut some of her hair off. It might be better to ask Jane to come in and cut it all off beforehand. In a proper style, you know, so that it looks as if it was meant to be like that. Do you think Jane would mind?"

Jane was a friend of Mum's who came round to the house to cut Tom's and Sophie's hair.

"Oh, Sarah," said Dad. "I'm sure she'd do it. I'll ring her, if you like."

"But she's been growing it for ages," said Tom without thinking. "She wouldn't want to have it all cut off."

"I know she wouldn't *want* to," said Mum, "I'm not stupid. But—"

"Perhaps she won't have to," interrupted Dad. "Let's wait and see. When will we know?"

"The neurosurgeons have a meeting tomorrow. Sort of a conference. They'll look at the results of the angiogram and then they'll decide."

"Tomorrow?"

"Yes. The nurse said they'd definitely let us know by the end of the day."

"Right. Not long to wait then. We'll come in again tomorrow, won't we, Tom?" He smiled at Tom and then turned back to Mum. "Where are you sleeping now? You look tired."

"Oh, I'll be living in luxury tonight," she said, smiling. "There's a spare bed in the parents' room. Should be better than a mattress in the play-room!"

As they left, Tom glanced back. The main lights were off. A lamp was on behind Sophie's bed. She lay still and peaceful in the pool of soft golden light. His father stood holding the door open, looking back at Sophie. He looked lost and sad, and he seemed as if he'd forgotten what he was doing. But then he sort of shook himself and smiled at Tom, and they walked up the long corridor, which was busy in the daytime but shadowed and silent now, and out into the night. Rain fell softly onto Tom's face. The hospital lights were blurred and wobbly, and he had to blink to clear his eyes. It was a very quiet journey home.

The next day, he felt heavy with tiredness. He sat in maths, gazing out of the window. It was windy and the sky was full of movement, with small swift charcoal coloured-clouds racing desperately ahead of great billowing piles of pale grey cumulus, as if they were trying to escape. A picture kept worming its way into his mind, of Sophie lying on an operating table, surrounded by doctors and nurses in green masks and caps and overalls. How would they get inside her head, he wondered? And how could they be sure they'd get it right, whatever it was they were thinking of doing? What if the knife slipped? Would that make it worse?

"Tom? Tom?" He jumped. Mr MacDonald – Big Mac – was looming over him, holding a pile of papers. "Your homework, please."

"Oh. Sorry, sir. I haven't done it. We were up at the hospital last night and—"

"Yes, yes, I see," cut in Mr MacDonald, looking embarrassed. "That's all right, I understand. Just do it when you can." Then he turned to Ashley Fox.

"Right, Ashley. What's your excuse this week?" he demanded.

"Just forgot. Sorry, sir."

"*Forgot?* Tell me, Ashley, which night do we have maths homework?"

"Don't know, sir."

"You don't know? Natalie, tell him."

"Tuesdays, sir."

"Tuesdays, yes. Thank you, Natalie. And how long have we been having maths homework on Tuesdays, Natalie?"

Natalie looked slightly worried. "All year, sir."

"All year. The same day every week. You'll find it written in the back of your homework book, Ashley. And yet, despite all this, you forgot. See me here at 1.30. And make sure you remember *that*, Ashley, because my patience is fast running out. And I'm not the only one, from what I hear in the staff room."

With a final glare, Mr MacDonald moved on. Ashley's eyes slid sideways to Tom, who felt a bit uncomfortable. They'd known each other since playschool. At one time, when they were small, they'd been quite friendly. Ashley had been to Tom's house – only once – and Tom had been back to Ashley's. There'd been a sandpit and they'd played with tractors and diggers, and pretended it was a quarry. But though they'd still played together at school, the friendship had fizzled out after a while – Tom couldn't really remember why. These days, Ashley was one of those people who always seemed to be in trouble, but it didn't seem to bother him. He was very good at playing the clown.

After the lesson, they were the last two in the classroom. Ashley was stuffing his books into his bag. Tom hesitated. Then he said, "I'm sorry about before. I mean, about MacDonald letting me off and having a pop at you. It wasn't fair, really. He was just nicer to me because of my sister."

"It's all right," said Ashley cheerfully. "I heard about her. She's ill, isn't she?"

"Yes. She might have to have an operation. On her brain. They're deciding today."

"No way! What's the matter with her? My Mum said she had a stroke, but that's something old people have, isn't it? Mr Parkinson down the road had one, then he had another one and then he – oh, sorry."

"It's all right," said Tom. It was actually a relief for someone to say what they were thinking, instead of tiptoeing around looking embarrassed. "The doctors say it's different when you're young. You get better quicker because your body's still growing, so it can mend itself faster."

"Oh. Well, that's not so bad then, is it? *Is* she getting better?"

Tom thought. "Well, I suppose she is a bit," he said doubtfully. "She can lift her foot up. She couldn't do that to start off with."

Mum had been thrilled about that a few days ago. She'd come hurrying to tell them, her face all lit up.

"Can't she walk, then?" asked Ashley.

"No. She's in a wheelchair. But they take her down to a gym every day and they're going to teach her how to walk again. Suppose she'll be able to soon."

"So what's this operation for, then?"

"Not sure. Dad says they might have to do something to her brain." Tom looked at Ashley. He wanted to explain how he felt, but he wasn't sure where he should start, or even whether Ash would want to listen.

"It's difficult," he said suddenly. "People think they know how you feel – like Mr MacDonald. But they don't. *I* don't even know."

His eyes were smarting, but he didn't want to wipe them in case Ashley thought he was crying. It

was all right, though, because Ashley wasn't looking – he was busy rummaging in his bag.

"Look!" he said triumphantly. "I've got my
football – do you want to go on the field?"

They went right to the far end of the football
pitch, as far away from the school buildings as
possible. A small river divided the playing fields
from the churchyard on the other side, and the
ground was soggy and squashy. Ashley shot the
ball across. Tom wasn't normally much good at
football, but today he felt exhilarated and
inspired, as if he could run for ever and never be
out of breath. He stopped the ball, controlling it
so precisely that it felt as if it was stuck to his toes.
Then he swooped off down the field till Ashley
charged across, swiped it away, and hurtled off
back to his goal, the vicarage wall. Tom raced
after him and did a flying tackle that would have
had the England crowd cheering. They rolled in
the mud, each struggling for possession, but it was
Tom who emerged triumphant. Breathless, he
glanced at his goal, a pile of coats and bags that
seemed miles away.

"Run!" he muttered fiercely to himself. "Run
like the wind!"

He felt strong and light and balanced. He felt
sure that if he'd wanted to, he could have stepped

onto the wind and used it as a staircase to the sky. But instead, he put all his magical power into hurtling towards his goal. He had never run so fast or felt so good.

Ash appeared beside him. "Where did that come from?" he asked, impressed. "Never knew you could run like that."

"Nor me," gasped Tom. "Nor me."

"Come on then – let's see how good you really are!" Ash grabbed the ball and pelted off with it.

They only stopped when they heard a distant bell and realized that it was the end of lunchtime.

"Oops," said Ash, hand to mouth, gazing at Tom.

"What?" said Tom. "...Oh!" They were both splattered with mud. Their shoes were covered, and there were thick patches on their trousers and shirts, and smears on their faces and in their hair. They burst out laughing and then hurried back into school, trying to brush the worst of it off. Then suddenly Ash stopped. There was a look of dismay on his face.

"Oh no!"

"What?" asked Tom.

"I've just remembered – I was supposed to see Big Mac at 1.30!"

"What are you going to do?" asked Tom.

"Dunno," said Ash.

They looked at each other.

"We could bunk off," suggested Tom.

"Where to?" asked Ash.

"Doesn't matter, does it? Anywhere. We might as well – we'll only get into trouble if we go back into school." Suddenly Tom felt brave and reckless.

Ash looked at him, surprised. "Yeah. But they'd know. Straightaway, when we weren't at registration. Big Mac would come looking for me, and I'd be in more trouble than ever."

"Oh. S'pose." Tom felt stupid. He hadn't thought of that.

"If you're going to walk out," explained Ash kindly, "you do it when no one will notice. No, we'll have to go in. But it's OK. They won't go on at you, because of your sister. And I'm used to it."

And they trudged in to face what they had to, leaving trails of muddy footprints along the corridor.

There was no one in when Tom got home. He had a big bowl of cornflakes with masses of milk and several spoonfuls of sugar, and wondered what to do about his uniform.

He changed his clothes and pushed his shirt deep down into the laundry basket. But he would need his trousers tomorrow. He took them downstairs and looked at the washing machine. He'd never used it before, but surely it couldn't be that difficult. He looked doubtfully at it. There was a row of switches and a dial with lots of numbers. How on earth were you supposed to know which number to start at? It was stupid. He gave up on that and moved the breakfast dishes out of the sink. He filled it with warm water and sloshed in some soap powder. Then he dumped the trousers in and swirled them about experimentally. Clouds of mud drifted into the water. That had to be good. Encouraged, he pounded them up and down energetically, which made drops of dirty water splash all over the draining board, the dishes, the wall and the window.

"Blast," he muttered. "Blast and damn."

He emptied the water out, filled the sink with more, and squeezed and kneaded the trousers again. More mud came out. He carried on till the water turned reasonably clear.

After he'd wrung them out as well as he could, he draped them over a radiator. They left a drippy trail on the carpet, but there wasn't much he could do about that. He went back into the kitchen to clear up the mess.

It was at that point that his father came home. He put his briefcase down and dropped his keys on the table.

"Hi, Tom," he said. "Had a good day?" He went over and switched the kettle on. Then he saw the muddy splashes. He peered at them. "Oh," he said. "What happened here?"

"Sorry, Dad," said Tom nervously, "I was just going to clear up."

"Oh. Well, that's all right then. Jolly good." He yawned and picked up a mug. He peered at it, frowned, rinsed it out and put a teabag in it.

"Put some water in that when it's boiled, will you? I'd better go up and get changed. We'll have to go to the hospital soon to find out about this operation."

When he'd gone upstairs, Tom stood there, his hands dangling at his sides. He felt flat. If it had been Mum, she'd have wanted to know why he'd had to wash his trousers out, how they'd got muddy, who he'd been with when it happened – she would have teased the whole story out of him, more surely than any TV policeman. And then she'd have told him off. It wasn't that he was looking for a telling off from Dad – of course he wasn't. But at least it would have shown that Dad actually spared him a thought from time to time.

"I'm not invisible," he muttered angrily. "I do exist. There's Sophie, but there's me as well." He threw the dishcloth into the sink and went upstairs to fetch his trainers. He stared out of his bedroom window. The clouds had partially cleared, and the rays of the evening sun shone down, rich and strangely brilliant. The Willow Man stood out against the flaming sky.

"Go on," Tom muttered, "don't just stand there. Do something. Do anything. Else what's the point of you?"

Then Dad called up the stairs and it was time to go.

Pairs

Sophie lay propped up in bed. Her mother had gone off somewhere with one of the other mums. It was a relief, really. She fussed too much. Everyone was always on at Sophie to do things. They wanted her to use her right hand. The occupational therapist was the worst. She had all these games – a giant drafts set, skittles, three-dimensional noughts and crosses – which she tried to persuade Sophie to play. Sophie would have humoured her if she could have used her left hand. But no, it always had to be her right one. Couldn't they all see it was useless? It wouldn't do what she told it to – it just lay there. It wasn't part of her any more. Why were they so stupid? Why couldn't they all just leave her alone?

And she was so tired, so sleepy all the time. It was much easier to watch a video – to watch the same one, over and over. The funny, fantastical

Flintstones, living their unreal lives in their unreal world. They came so close to disaster, but they always managed to evade it in the end. You knew that Fred would triumph. You knew that, in the end, everything would be all right.

She must have drifted off, because she gradually became aware that someone was beside the bed saying her name. Irritated, she opened her eyes. But it was Hannah, the nice nurse. She liked Hannah. She was pretty and fun, and she never nagged or looked worried.

"Come on," said Hannah, "let's have you in this wheelchair. I'll take you down to the other end of the ward and we'll see what's going on."

Later, she helped Sophie to sit up and turn so she was sitting on the edge of the bed. Then all she had to do was slide down off the bed, shuffle a bit and flop into the chair. "Brilliant!" said Hannah. "There's just one thing."

Sophie looked at her, puzzled. "Duh! Your arm!" said Hannah. "You have got two, you know. Ha! I've got an idea. Let's get your dog. He's like the one in that film, isn't he? You know, *Beethoven*. Is that who he's meant to be?"

Sophie hadn't thought of it. She never gave her toys names and was always a bit stumped when grownups asked what they were called. But she'd liked the film, and she liked Hannah, so she had a go at smiling. It felt funny, and she wondered what it looked like. She couldn't remember the last time she'd smiled. There hadn't been a whole lot to smile about, really.

"Excellent!" beamed Hannah. "There, now, you can rest your arm on Beethoven. Then you're looking after him and he's looking after you. OK?"

Sophie smiled again. It felt less odd the second time.

There was a table at the other end of the ward, and shelves stacked with games and books. A boy was sitting there in a wheelchair. He was quite a bit older than her, probably about Tom's age. He had a pack of cards laid out in front of him in lines and he was peering at them thoughtfully. She wondered what was wrong with him. He looked pale, but both sides of his face seemed to be working. So he couldn't have had a stroke. She hadn't seen any other children who'd had one. There were people in the gym where she had physio who'd had strokes, but they were mostly old.

"Sophie's come to play cards," said Hannah, "but she can only use one hand. Oh, and she can't talk at the moment either. This is Ben, Sophie."

Ben looked pleased. "Oh, great! I'm fed up with playing Patience. What shall we play? Do you know how to play pairs? You pick two cards up," he explained, "and if they're the same – like two tens, or two Queens – you get to keep them. If they're not the same, you put them down again and it's the other person's turn. The person who ends up with most pairs wins."

The first two Sophie picked up were not a pair – they were a three of hearts and a seven of clubs. But she put them down carefully and remembered where they were. The next time it was her turn, they weren't the same either. But the time after that, one was a three of diamonds. Her left hand went straight to the three of hearts she'd picked up earlier. This was easy.

Ben was good at remembering where the cards were, but she was better. She won easily. She smiled a much bigger smile. She needed to speak. She tried to remember how to do it. You had to kind of open your lips, and then push them together, and then let the breath out, as if you were blowing a kiss. She concentrated, hard.

"More!" she said. "More!"

Hannah was still there, watching. She jumped. "You spoke!" she said. "You did it!" She hugged Sophie. "That's so brilliant!"

Sophie's mother and father and Tom were just walking into the ward. They were excited when Hannah told them that Sophie had said something. But Sophie didn't want a fuss. She wanted to carry on playing cards. They really shouldn't interrupt. She ignored them and looked at Ben. "More," she commanded again.

Tom's mum was thrilled that Sophie had spoken. She and Tom and Dad had been having a meal together in the hospital café. She was already excited, because the neurosurgeons had been to talk to her about the results of Sophie's tests; they had told her that Sophie wouldn't need an operation after all – her brain was mending itself. When the clot had blocked the artery in her neck the blood hadn't been able to get past, and so a bit of her brain had been starved of oxygen and died. That was why her right side had stopped working: it wasn't getting the messages from her brain that told it what to do. The neurosurgeons had thought they might have to use some other blood vessels to bypass the dead bit, but it turned out they didn't need to. Sophie's brain had already activated some that were just idling around not doing anything, and they were taking over from the damaged ones.

Tom felt relieved. Perhaps now things would start to get back to normal.

His mother and father had talked and talked over the meal, about whether they would need a ramp for the wheelchair, what to do about school – even about whether they'd be able to go on holiday in the summer. Mum had been excited and happy. And now there was more good news – Sophie could speak again.

When the game had finished, Mum knelt down beside Sophie. "Say it again, Sophie! Say it for me!"

Sophie gazed at her. She moved her lips, concentrating.

"M – Mummm!" And she gave a funny, lopsided smile.

Mum looked as if she'd had Christmas and her birthday all in one, with extra icing and sugar sprinkles, and Dad smiled broadly.

Tom watched. They'd forgotten about him. He understood it perfectly – Sophie had been really ill, and now she was starting to get better and that was great. But he just didn't know where he fitted in. They used to be a square – Mum and Dad, him and Sophie – but now it was more like a triangle. An isosceles one, with Mum and Dad at the bottom, always peering anxiously up at Sophie, balanced in between, always in the spotlight – while Tom hovered uneasily on the outside.

He glanced at the boy in the wheelchair. He'd never seen him before, but even so, he seemed to be more involved than Tom was. Perhaps the boy felt his gaze, because he turned and looked at Tom.

He seemed to be about to speak, but then Sophie banged on the table and pointed to the cards. The boy laughed and glanced at Tom again. "Do you want to play as well?" he said.

"No, thanks," said Tom politely, "I'm not very good at cards."

He went into the playroom. There was no one in there. There usually wasn't. He switched on the TV. It was *EastEnders*. Mum didn't like him watching it – she said it was just a lot of nasty people yelling at each other. She was right. He settled down and listened to the angry voices. It was something for him to do.

The next day, he found himself walking out of class with Ash and telling him about Sophie beginning to get better and coming home. It was odd, really. He couldn't talk to his old friends about what had happened. They seemed to belong to another life: he wouldn't know how to start to talk to them or what words to use. But there was something about Ash that made it easier. Perhaps it was to do with him being an outsider too. Because they were outsiders, both of them, though for different reasons. Tom was outside everyday life now, in a place where bad things happened, and he somehow knew that Ash was too, and had been for a long time. The bad things were different for each of them – he didn't even know exactly what they were for Ash – but still, he felt at the moment that he had more in

38

common with him than with his old friends.

"Well," said Ash, "that's great, isn't it? So she'll come home soon, will she?"

"Yes," said Tom. "It'll be weekends for a bit, and then she'll come home for good, I suppose. Dunno, really. Anyway, what happened about you and MacDonald? What did he say?"

Ash shrugged. "Usual sort of stuff. Detention after school. Letter home to parents. Well, parent."

"Parent?"

"They don't seem to have noticed I've only got one. Well, only one that counts, anyway. Dad left years ago, when Matthew was a baby. Matthew's my brother," he added.

They were sitting on the wall beside the road that led into school. It was a popular spot at break time for people to sit and eat sandwiches or crisps. A group of boys Tom was friendly with were kicking a ball about – one or two of them looked at him curiously. They were probably wondering what he was doing with Ash. Tom felt hungry. There hadn't been anything in the house that he could bring for a snack. A girl from his class was sitting nearby. She had a plastic box packed with carefully wrapped rolls, and a chocolate bar and a satsuma. Ash saw him looking at the food.

"Here, I've got a Mars bar," he said. "Want some?"

Tom took it gratefully.

"When is it?" asked Tom.

"What?"

"Your detention."

"Oh. Next week."

"It's not fair. You didn't do anything I didn't do."

"No. Well, that's just the way it is. Doesn't matter. It's OK." They concentrated on the chocolate for a bit and then Ash said, "We could play football again later. If you want."

"Yeah, all right," said Tom. Then he asked shyly, "What are you doing on Saturday?"

"Nothing special. Why?"

"Dunno. Thought maybe we could do something."

"Could do. All right, then. I'll call for you."

The bell went, and as Tom went up to the history room, he remembered that Sophie was coming home that weekend for the first time. He frowned. Still, it probably didn't matter. In fact, it might be easier if he was out of the way. Let's face it, he thought, most probably no one will even notice whether I'm there or not. Well, anyway, he'd arranged it now. Maybe they could go for a walk, go exploring somewhere. Ash might be able to think of some good places to go. The image of the Willow Man strode into his thoughts and seemed to turn its sightless eyes towards him.

That was a thought. They could go and see the Willow Man. There was something about it, something that drew him. He'd like a closer look at it. Anyway, it would be somewhere to go.

Ash had to hurry at the end of school. His mum's friend Gina usually collected Matthew from the first school with her own son, Kieran: they were good friends and she only lived a couple of streets away. But on Fridays, Gina took Kieran swimming, so Ash had to get there before four-fifteen to pick Matthew up.

"Wish I was going swimming," said Matthew as they walked home.

Ash glanced at him. The swimming baths were on the other side of town. It was too far to walk, and there wasn't a bus – really, you needed a car to get there. He'd been once or twice when he was smaller. People used to go there for birthday parties – he might even have gone with Tom once.

"I'll take you one day," he offered. "In the holidays. We'll go on an expedition."

Matthew brightened. "Will we take supplies – chocolate and sweets and stuff?"

"Course. Wouldn't be an expedition without supplies."

He told Matthew what it would be like, describing the chutes and the splashing and the noise, and the burgers they'd have afterwards. By the time he'd finished, they were home, and Harry was making an ecstatic fuss of them. Ash got drinks and biscuits – dog ones for Harry, digestives for him and Matthew. Mum would be home soon. She was always in a good mood on a Friday because she didn't work weekends – not usually, anyway. Often she brought home treats for tea.

And then, tomorrow he was meeting Tom. It was quite unusual for him to be seeing a friend at the weekend. He used to play with friends when he was little, the same as Matthew did, but it happened less and less as he got older. Some of them were busy with football practice, that kind of thing. Maybe you had to have a dad to get you into all that. It had never happened for him, anyway.

He settled down in front of the television. When Mum came home, he'd take Harry for a walk. It hadn't been a bad week, really. Well, apart from the run-in with Big Mac, and he was used to that kind of thing – he just didn't have a way with teachers like some people did. People like Tom, for instance. Mind you, Tom had other problems... Ash glanced over at Matthew. He was a pain in the neck sometimes – well, often – but it would be awful if he was really ill, like Sophie.

Crushed

It was Friday, so Tom's dad came home early. He looked round the kitchen as if he'd never seen it before, and frowned.

"I think we'd better have a bit of a tidy up," he said. "I don't think your mother will be too impressed if she comes home and sees this lot." Tom looked round. There were dirty dishes in the sink, saucepans on top of the cooker, half-empty milk bottles on the table.

"Tell you what," said Dad. "I'll do the kitchen, and you get the vacuum cleaner out and tackle the living room. We'll have to be quick; we've got to fetch them soon."

After fifteen minutes they thought they'd finished. Tom looked around, pleased. There didn't seem to be any obvious dirt, all the newspapers were tidied up, and you could see the table again. Mum wouldn't need to sigh and look tired, or frown and get cross. They'd done a good job. But Dad still wasn't quite satisfied.

"Flowers," he said. "I should have got some flowers. Is there anything in the garden? Can you have a quick look, see if you can find anything, while I get changed?"

It was already starting to get dark. Tom looked round. He could see nothing promising. It was still winter; there were a few purple and yellow crocuses, but they were too small to pick.

Then he noticed a flash of colour. He knelt down. It was a bud, slim and pointed, with furled silvery petals tipped with a pale, clear lavender blue. There were two other smaller ones, nestling in a clump of spiky green leaves. He picked them and found a narrow glass vase in the cupboard by the front door. He put them in the centre of the table and stood back to admire them.

"Brilliant!" said his father. "They're really pretty, aren't they? Right, I think that's it – no, wait. Your mother always leaves a lamp on. She says it's more welcoming when you come in." He looked at Tom. "You've done a great job. Thank you." He paused and said awkwardly, "It's not been easy, has it? But the worst bit's over now. Sophie *will* get better. It'll just take time."

Tom wasn't sure the flowers were properly in

the middle of the table. He moved them slightly, carefully.

"Dad," he said.

"Yes?"

"The stroke," said Tom. "Why did it happen?"

Dad looked puzzled. "You know why. Because of the clot. It blocked—"

"Yes," said Tom in a rush, "but – she was all upset just before it. Was that—?"

Dad's face cleared. "Nothing to do with it. Absolutely nothing. The clot was there, and it was going to get stuck. No one could have known, and there was nothing anyone could have done about it."

Tom felt deeply relieved. It hadn't been his fault. He'd never really thought it was, but it felt good to be sure.

"All right?" said Dad.

Tom nodded.

"Come on, then. Let's go and fetch them home."

They brought Sophie up the path in the wheelchair. The front step was too steep for it, so Dad picked her up and carried her inside. Tom and Mum followed.

When they came into the living room, Mum stopped and looked round. "Oh, it *is* good to be home! It's all so tidy – and you found some irises! Look, Sophie!"

Sophie smiled her lopsided smile, and her father put her down on the settee, propping her up carefully with cushions.

"There are more presents for you," he said. "Aren't you the lucky one? One of my classes sent this." It was a large dog. It wasn't floppy, like Beethoven; it was heavy and solid and sitting up alertly. Its gleaming dark eyes were edged with thick dark lashes, not at all like a real dog's, but very pretty. There was a big card with it, and the class had all written their names inside. Some had done drawings as well. They'd gone to a lot of trouble. Sophie hardly looked at the card, and Dad looked as if he was going to ask her why not, but caught Mum's eye and didn't.

"And then there's this," he said. It was a game from someone in the village, something to do with words. There were counters with letters on them. Sophie sifted through them. Then she pushed the game away. She turned back to the dog, stroking her cheek on its soft velvet coat. Then she looked round anxiously. "B...B...?" she said.

"Oh," said Mum, "you mean Beethoven. He's here, on top of the bag." She passed him to Sophie, who clutched him to her and then looked pointedly at the television. Mum laughed.

"All right," she said. "Tom, can you choose a video for Sophie? I don't think there'd be anything on at the moment that she'd want to watch. Find something she likes."

Tom chose *The Lion King*. Meanwhile, his mother had gone into the kitchen and was busy wiping work surfaces and putting things away.

"What are you doing?" said his father, sounding annoyed. "You don't need to be fussing about in here. Go and sit down, relax. It's all organized, you don't have to worry. I've got some pizzas. Tom'll bring you a drink." He shooed her out, got a bottle of wine from the fridge and told Tom to get a wine glass out while he opened the bottle. By the time he'd poured it out and Tom had carried it carefully through to the living room, Mum was leaning back in her chair, her eyes closed. The lions prowled sweetly across the screen, shaking their floppy manes, blinking their large cartoon eyes.

Tom set the table. It was long and narrow, and there wasn't much space in the middle for everything that needed to go on it. He looked critically at the chairs, wondering if they would be safe. Sophie couldn't sit up very well by herself yet – she needed to be supported. Then he saw the chair over by the desk. The back curved round to form encircling arms – that would be better. He lugged it over and put a cushion on it.

Sophie smiled when she saw the pizza.

"Put your arm on the table," said Mum. "Don't just forget about it – remember what Rachel said!"

Sophie stopped smiling.

"Who's Rachel?" asked Tom.

"The occupational therapist up at the hospital. She's a bit fierce. She keeps telling Sophie she mustn't forget about her right hand. She's got to try and do things with it to get it to work again."

Sophie scowled. Tom had put her glass of water on the right of her plate, as usual, forgetting that she couldn't use that hand any more. Sophie reached over for it with her left hand. As she did so, she caught the vase of flowers. The glass shattered and the water made a puddle, then a stream, then a waterfall off the edge of the table. Mum leapt up and Dad rushed in from the kitchen.

"It's all right, don't worry, we'll soon have it cleared up," said Dad. While they fussed about with dishcloths and dustpans, Tom watched Sophie. She had never been clumsy. She had always been good with her hands – always drawing, always fashioning things out of paper and bits of material and glue. Now she was gazing at the flowers, which were lying on the table intermingled with fragments of glass. They had begun to open up since they had been inside. They were blue and beautiful, fragile

48

and soft. Sophie reached out and touched one.

"Watch out!" said Mum quickly. "You'll cut yourself!"

Sophie carefully picked up the flower. She looked at it for a moment, and then her fingers closed round it tighter and tighter, and she crushed it. And the look on her face made Tom wish that there was something – anything – he could do to make it all better. Not in a few weeks or months or years – but now.

The Angel of the South

"You want to go and see the Willow Man?" said Ash, staring.

"Well, no," said Tom, "not if you don't want to. I just thought, you know, it'd be somewhere to go."

"So would school on a Saturday," pointed out Ash, "but it doesn't mean we have to go there."

"I know, but I'd just like to see how it's made, that's all, and what it looks like close up. There's – I dunno. There's just something about it."

"OK," said Ash cheerfully. "Whatever."

It was a bright, cold day. Ash had brought his dog, Harry.

"Short for Harrier. Harrier jump jets. You know – vertical take-off planes. We went to Yeovilton once – they have planes there, only it's the navy, not the RAF. They have these jets that take off straight up into the air. My dad took us."

"Your dad?"

"Yes. Before he left."

"Oh." Tom thought a bit. "But why did you call a dog after a plane?"

"You'll see. He's a brilliant dog. Aren't you, Harry? Come on then – which way is it?"

"Umm," said Tom.

"You do know how we get there, don't you?" asked Ash.

"Well," said Tom defensively, "I've only ever seen it from the motorway. I don't know how you actually get there – but it can't be that difficult."

Ash sighed. "Well, the motorway's over that way – listen, you can hear it. I should think if we cut through the estate and down past Foxholes Farm we ought to be somewhere near it."

They went past rows of houses. Tom knew Ash's house was on the estate – he remembered going there when they were little, but he couldn't remember much about it, except that there was a sandpit in the back garden, where they'd played with their tractors and diggers. He wondered how long Ash's dad had been gone and why he'd left. It wasn't the kind of thing you could ask, though, so he didn't.

When they'd gone past the houses, Ash let Harry off the lead and fished a ball out of his pocket. Harry's ears pricked up: he quivered with excitement. "Here!" said Ash.

He held the ball high above his head. Harry leapt up, straight up in the air, trying to reach it.

"There!" said Tom. "A vertical take-off! That's why he's a Harrier. Did you ever see a dog do that? It's brilliant, isn't it? You're a mad dog, aren't you? Mad!" He threw the ball and Harry hurtled after it, reaching it at the same time as it hit the ground. "He's better with a ball than you'll ever be. Or me."

"Look!" said Tom. "There it is!"

It was the Willow Man. They could glimpse it through a gap between two farm buildings.

"It looks different from here," said Tom thoughtfully, "almost as if it was dancing. And there's something funny about its head."

"A bird," grinned Ash, "that's all. It's got a bird sitting on its head. Cheeky, eh?"

It stood alone in the middle of a large field. They climbed over the fence and went up to it. The sun shone in a blue crystal sky, and the figure etched a long sharp shadow on the grass.

"Doesn't look as if it's dancing now," said Ash. It looked huge – more powerful than ever. As he gazed up at it, a trail of cloud appeared from nowhere and cut across the sun. He followed it with his eyes. The Willow Man reared high above him. The sun came back from behind the cloud, dazzling and triumphant. The sky was spinning. He stepped back, shaken.

"Do you think it's real?" he whispered, gazing up at the proud, outstretched arms.

"Real? What do you mean, real? Of course it's real. You can touch it, see?" Tom reached out. But he didn't touch it. Not quite.

"I don't mean that kind of real."

Harry whined softly. He wouldn't go near the figure.

"He doesn't like it," said Ash.

"It's beautiful," said Tom. "I think it's beautiful."

"Beautiful?" Ash seemed to turn the word round and round, examine it and then reject it. "It's strong," he said. "Look how strong it is."

Another cloud passed over the sun. The golden afternoon turned to steel. Ash shivered.

"I brought some chocolate," said Tom. "Want some?"

"Yes," said Ash, "but not here."

They began to walk back. Then Ash spoke.

"Why is it there?"

"I don't know. I suppose they needed a big flat field – and maybe they wanted it to be near the motorway so lots of people would see it."

"No, I mean – why did anyone want to put it anywhere? Why was it made at all?"

Tom remembered reading a newspaper article when the figure was being built. He told Ash about it.

"It said there's another one up north somewhere, called the Angel of the North. This is a
kind of Angel of the South."

"An angel? It's an angel? Is the other one the
same?"

"Don't think so." Tom had a vague memory of
a picture of something that was all angles, something hard and metallic, something winged. "No,
not the same at all, really. But big. Bigger even
than this one, I think."

"Do you think it's an angel?"

Tom wasn't sure what an angel might be like.
Maybe it was one. But then he thought of something.

"It doesn't have wings, does it? I don't see how
it can be an angel if it doesn't have wings."

"Is that what makes an angel? What about
being good? Doesn't an angel have to be good?"
demanded Ash.

Tom looked at Ash in surprise. This was getting
a bit deep. All he really knew about angels was
from Christmas: angels on cards, on top of the
Christmas tree, in picture books – beautiful crea-
tures with long golden curls and strange eyes, with
tunics and matching haloes in shades of amber,
gold and chalky rose, kneeling down beside Mary
to tell her she was going to have a bit of a shock in
a few months' time.

"Dunno," he said. "Haven't met many. There's not much call for them round here, is there?" He wrestled the ball from Ash, threw it for Harry, then swooped after him as he ran down the lane, arms flapping up and down, a dive-bombing angel. "I'm an angel! Nyaaoow! Nyaaoow!"

Ash laughed and the afternoon lightened. But later, as they neared the village, he returned to the subject.

"All the same, though," he said, "there's something weird about the Willow Man. There is, you know it. Else why did you want to go there?"

Tom tried to think.

"I don't think there's anything wrong about it. I just like it because it's—" He'd said it was beautiful when they were near it, but that wasn't a word he could use again, not now they were back in their ordinary everyday lives. He searched for other words. "It's so strong, and yet it can't move." Like Sophie, he thought. He remembered she was at home and felt guilty. Perhaps he should be at home, helping.

The sun was sinking and turning red, and it was colder. They walked back quickly and without saying very much.

The house was warm and smelt of roasting chicken. It felt like home again. His mother was sitting in the kitchen with a cup of tea and the paper. She smiled at him.

"Good walk?"

"Yes, thanks," he said.

"Where'd you go?"

"Oh – you know." He grinned. She knew perfectly well he wouldn't tell her. It had been Sophie's habit to come in and tell Mum the story of her day – who she'd played with, what she'd done in school, what the teacher had said – but Tom had always believed in keeping things properly separate, not giving away too much. Mum still asked, though – it was a sort of game, one she didn't expect to win, but enjoyed playing.

"Who was that who called for you?" she asked casually.

"Ashley," he said. "Ashley Fox."

"Not one of your usual friends, is he?"

He shrugged.

"Have you been seeing much of him?"

He looked at her. She was breaking the rules, wanting to know too much. Why? What had she heard about Ash?

"A bit. Why?"

"Oh, nothing. Just wondered."

She went back to her newspaper.

Annoyed, he went in to see Sophie. They played pairs. Sophie won every game. At first it was funny, but then that was annoying too.

"How does she do it?" he said. "She remembers every single card. It's weird."

Sophie looked triumphant and punched the air with her left hand.

"I'll take you on," said Dad.

Tom left them to it and went up to his room. He went over to the window to close the curtains. The moon was huge and pale. On second thoughts, he shut the door, switched the light off again and left the curtains open. The pale silvery light streamed in. He lay on the bed and listened to the silence.

Talking to the Man

And so there was a new pattern to the week. From Friday to Sunday they were all together. During the week Sophie and Mum stayed up at the hospital so that Sophie could have regular physio. Tom and Dad didn't visit in the week any more – it was a long way, and it didn't seem to make much difference to Sophie whether they went or not. In fact, Tom sometimes felt as if they were interrupting things when they did go: even Mum always seemed as if she had plenty to do, chatting to the other mums and stuff.

It was all right at home. They ate pizzas a lot, and pies and chips, and anything else that was quick and easy; Dad caught up with his school-work, and Tom did just enough homework to keep out of trouble.

At school, Tom and Ash began to sit together in class. One morning Ash was late. There was nothing unusual about that – but this time he was *really* late. Mr Fieldhouse, their tutor, said he would have to go and get a late slip.

"Another one of those, Ashley, and you'll be having a detention, I'm afraid," said Mr Fieldhouse, looking at Ash thoughtfully over the top of his glasses. "Put your tie on properly and tuck your shirt in, or you'll be in trouble for that as well."

Ashley did as he was told and went off to the office. He did look even scruffier than usual. But that wasn't what Tom noticed. It was the look in his eyes and the way his shoulders were slumped.

"What's up?" whispered Tom anxiously in the first lesson, which was maths.

"Nothing," muttered Ash. "Tell you later."

"You two!" snapped Mr MacDonald. "The idea is that when I'm talking, you listen! Got that? It's really not so very difficult. Right – let's get on, then!"

Big Mac always seemed to notice when Ash was talking. In fact, he often thought Ash was talking even when he wasn't. If there was a disturbance while Big Mac had his back to the class because he was writing on the whiteboard, he would always turn round and accuse Ash or one of a couple of other boys he seemed to have it in for. Like later on that lesson. People started talking, and Big Mac whirled round, looking to see who it was.

"Ashley Fox!" he roared. "How many more

times! It's not as if you find maths easy, is it? I'd say that you needed to concentrate more than most. I just don't understand your attitude, I really don't."

Normally, Ash would greet such an outburst with a grin as soon as Mac turned back to the board, but today his face turned white and stony.

At break Ash and Tom went for a walk round the edge of the football field. It was out of bounds for playing because of the mud.

"The letter from school came," said Ash. "You know, about last week. Mum went mad." His face was pale and miserable. Tom didn't know what to say. Of course she would go mad. So would his mum – so would any mum.

"And that made us late," went on Ash. "And I have to take Matthew to school, because Mum's got a job in a shop and it's really important for her to keep it."

"Why shouldn't she be able to keep it?" asked Tom, puzzled.

"She won't keep it if she keeps being late. We haven't got a car, so she has to get a bus. And if she takes Matthew into school first she'll miss it. So that's why I take him. And usually it's all right, but if something goes wrong, like if we can't find his PE kit – or I get a letter from school – I'm the one who's late, because his school's the opposite direction from ours."

"She'll probably have calmed down by tonight," suggested Tom.

Ash stopped and glared at Tom. "Maybe. But that won't stop me being late, will it? It won't stop me getting into trouble all the time. It's just not fair – why is it always me they pick on? It's never someone like you – nothing ever goes wrong for you!"

"Nothing ever goes wrong?" repeated Tom incredulously. *"Nothing ever goes wrong?"*

Ash stared at him. He opened his mouth to say something, but no words emerged. He turned on his heel and walked quickly off, his shoulders hunched and his hands jammed into his pockets.

It was games that afternoon. Tom saw Ash at the beginning, but he didn't see him again during the afternoon, not even in the changing rooms at the end.

Then as he walked home, Ash appeared beside him. He looked a mess, with muddy shoes and trousers, but his blue eyes were calm.

"Sorry," he said gruffly. "I shouldn't have said that. It wasn't what I meant."

"I know," said Tom. "I do know what you meant." And it was true, he did. When he'd thought about it, he'd understood. What had happened to Sophie had come out of the blue. But the bad stuff that happened to Ash was there all the time; it was part of his life.

"Where've you been?" said Tom. "You skived, didn't you?"

"Well, maybe. Just a bit."

"Where'd you go?"

"I went back to see that angel of yours." He grinned. "He's not gone anywhere, not yet. We had a bit of a chat. He said I was to say sorry to you – you never did anything, so I shouldn't have gone off at you. And he said skiving off school wouldn't help, either. Nosey old devil. Angel, I mean."

Tom smiled, a little unwillingly. "Nobody noticed you weren't there. Least, I'm pretty sure they didn't."

"It's what I told you before. You have to time it so they won't notice. You have to know what you're doing. But I won't skive again. Otherwise, that angel might come after me."

They decided to take Harry for a walk again the next Saturday, but they didn't go near the Willow Man. They played football with Harry on the rec, not noticing that it was beginning to rain, and when Tom got back his mother was furious.

"Look at the state of you! As if I haven't got enough to do without washing your muddy clothes – and those are your decent jeans! Why on earth don't you put your old ones on if you're just going to be mucking about?"

Things seemed to be getting back to normal, thought Tom. Since Sophie's stroke, everyone had been tiptoeing round being nice to each other. It was as if Mum and Dad were so full of this big thing that had happened that they wouldn't allow little things to annoy them; everyone had to be supportive and considerate. Except Sophie, of course, who could be as bad-tempered as she liked and still have everyone fluttering round anxiously and making excuses for her. She was watching one of her videos again. Well, if Mum was allowed to get cross about stupid things, that was fine – so could he.

"Can I watch the football?" he asked loudly.

Dad looked at him, surprised. "Sophie's watching something at the moment," he said.

"Yes," said Tom mutinously, "she always is, isn't she?"

Anger bubbled up inside him, fierce and violent. It wasn't a feeling he was used to, and he felt half excited by it and half frightened. If a volcano had feelings, he thought, maybe it would feel like this. But a volcano could erupt in fantastic technicolour freedom without having to bother about upsetting anyone. He couldn't do that. No one was allowed to snap at Sophie; she was off limits. Furiously, he stamped upstairs, slammed his door, put on the loudest CD he could find and turned up the volume. It wasn't a brilliant substitute, but it helped a bit.

Before long his mother was knocking at the door. He was more than prepared to defend his right to entertain himself, but it turned out not to be necessary; she'd just come to tell him that someone was on the phone for him.

"I think it's Richard Carpenter," she said, with her hands over her ears.

Richard wanted him to go over the next day to try out a new computer game. Mum liked Richard. She was friends with his mother. Tom didn't mind him, but he didn't particularly want to spend time with him at the moment, and for some reason he didn't feel in the least inclined to fit in with what his mother wanted.

"Thanks," said Tom, "but my sister's home and I think I should stay in and help – you know." He put the phone down.

His mother lifted an eyebrow.

"What?" he said. "I don't want to go out."

"You were happy enough to go out with Ashley Fox," she pointed out.

"So?"

"So," she said patiently, "what's wrong with Richard?"

"What's wrong with Ashley?"

She stared at him and turned away to the sink. He thought that whatever she was washing must be exceptionally clean by now, because she kept on scrubbing it, over and over again. He was in the wrong. He knew it. She thought he was being unreasonable. He sighed.

"I like Ash. We just get on. What's wrong with him?"

Her hands became still, and she took them out of the water and dried them carefully.

"You're right," she said. "There's nothing wrong with him. I just wondered why you'd stopped going round with Richard and the others, that's all. But that's your business. Next weekend, why don't you ask Ash round? We thought we'd go to Wivenhoe House, have a family day out. Maybe Ash would like to come too."

"Maybe," said Tom doubtfully. Spending a perfectly good Saturday trailing round a stately home certainly wasn't his idea of fun, and he couldn't see it appealing to Ash. Still, he could always say no. "All right, I'll ask him." He picked up the tea towel and began to dry the dishes.

"Peace?" she said

"I'll think about it."

She plunged her hands back into the water and swirled the bubbles about.

"I really need you not to be stroppy at the moment. I know you're nearly a teenager, and it's supposed to be allowed, but – not now. All right?"

It sounded fair enough. But it didn't *feel* fair.

Not Dancing but Waving

On Monday, Tom met up with Ash at lunchtime. He had been wondering whether Ash was still in trouble at home.

After they'd talked a bit about what they'd watched on TV over the weekend, he said to Ash, "So how's it going? Is your mum still mad?"

"Not exactly," said Ash. "But she's got to come into school on Wednesday to see Mr Wilson." Mr Wilson was the head of year. "She had to ask if she could change her shift, so she's not best pleased."

"What – she's got to come in just because you missed MacDonald's detention?"

"It's not just that," admitted Ash. "That wasn't the first one I've missed. There's been a couple of after-school ones as well."

"Oh," said Tom. After-school detentions were more serious.

"I can't stay behind," said Ash, "because I have to pick Matthew up."

"Can't you tell them that?"

"I've tried. They don't listen. You know how they are – they don't give you a chance. And then I get mad, and then – oh, you know."

A few weeks ago, Tom wouldn't have known about being angry. But he did now. He just had to think back to what he'd felt like on Saturday night, when he'd wanted to watch football and couldn't because of Sophie. He'd known then what it felt like to be so angry you couldn't put it into words.

The bell went. It was time to go in. Tom wanted to say something comforting, something that would show he understood.

"Maybe it'll be all right," he tried. They both contemplated this possibility.

"Yeah," said Ash. "Maybe."

And amazingly, it was. Ash came in early on Thursday morning. That was surprising enough. But on top of that, his shirt was tucked in and his shoes were not covered in mud.

"So how'd it go?" asked Tom.

"Not too bad. Not too bad at all. He didn't just go on about me, like I thought he would. Mum explained about her job and about Matthew, and

Mr Wilson listened to her, he really did. He told Mum there was a breakfast club at Matthew's school, and he rang the head there and sorted it out – so Mum can take Matthew into school before she goes to work, and he can have some breakfast if he wants, or they'll do stuff with him – you know. And he says he wants to see me once a week – but just to talk, not because I'm in trouble."

Ash thought about this. "What does he want to talk about?"

"No idea. But I don't mind. He's not like MacDonald. He doesn't shout."

"Oh. Well, that's all right, then." Tom remembered about Saturday. "My mum says would you like to come round on Saturday?"

"What, me?" Ash looked startled. "To your house?"

"Yes. Well, actually, I think she wants to go somewhere – you know, out for the day. If it's nice."

"Oh. Right – OK then. Cool."

Cool? A family day out at a stately home? Rooms full of boring pictures and furniture? Tom didn't think so. He really didn't. It might be Mum's idea of a relaxing day out, but it certainly wasn't his. All he could hope was that it wouldn't be too horribly embarrassing, and that afterwards Ash wouldn't dismiss him as a total loser from

Planet Middle Class. He sighed. There really was no end to things never being simple.

Saturday morning was dry and sunny, which, Tom supposed, could be either a good thing or make it even more of a wasted day, depending on which way you looked at it.

"Are we taking sandwiches?" asked Dad.

"Yes," said Mum. "It might be a bit tricky getting into the café with the wheelchair, don't you think?"

"Well, maybe. But I thought everywhere had to be wheelchair friendly these days. Won't it be cold for eating outside?"

"Hm. Well, we'll see. We can always go in for a hot drink, I suppose…"

Someone knocked on the door and Tom went to answer it. It was Ash. Tom led him in, feeling a bit self-conscious and wondering whether he would have to make proper introductions. But it was OK, because Ash went straight over to where Sophie sat in her wheelchair.

"Hello," he said. "I've brought you something – a card. I made it for you."

Sophie took it with her left hand and gazed at it. A smile crept over her face.

"The man," she said.

Tom went over to look. It had a picture of the

Willow Man on it. It was a very good drawing. But then he noticed something.

"It isn't our Willow Man, is it?" he said. "This one's dancing. Look, Sophie, he's waving his arms about." He looked at Ash, puzzled.

"It is ours," said Ash. "It's how he would be, if he could."

"Why, it's lovely," said Mum. "You're really good at drawing, Ashley."

Ash looked embarrassed. His eyes darted round, searching desperately for something which would distract everyone's attention. His gaze fell on Sophie's chair. "Hey, can I push?" he said.

Soon they were all in the car and heading down the motorway. Sophie was sitting between Tom and Ash. She was much better at sitting up than she had been last time Tom had been in the car with her. Then, she had kept slipping sideways, and in the end it had been easier to let her rest against his shoulder. It had been a bit uncomfortable until he'd thought to put his arm around her, but then it had been OK, and she'd gone to sleep.

But today she was looking out of the window and smiling.

"Look!" she said. "Waving!"

"Who is?" asked Mum.

"The Willow Man," said Ash. His voice sounded

a little odd. "Funny that. He really does look as if he's waving."

By the time Tom looked round, the figure had slid behind them and was shrinking. But he looked just the same as usual to Tom.

"Yeah, right!" he said, grinning at Ash.

"Was," said Sophie calmly. "Was waving."

When they reached Wivenhoe House, it was Ash who lifted the wheelchair out of the boot. He seemed fascinated by the way it worked, and knew without being told which bits needed to be pushed, pulled and tapped into place. Sophie had obviously taken to him, and she insisted that he should push the chair.

When they paid to go in, Tom's mum asked if the house was accessible for wheelchairs. The man looked apologetic.

"Not much of it is, I'm afraid. Just the ground floor. You won't be able to get down to the kitchens or up to the Long Gallery, and they're really the most interesting bits, specially for children."

"Oh, dear," said Mum, looking troubled. "I really should have rung up to check, shouldn't I? I'm so sorry, all of you."

Tom saw the opening and leapt through it in relief. "I know," he said. "Why don't you two go round the house, and me and Ash can take Sophie round the gardens?"

"Oh no," said his mother, "that wouldn't be fair – the house is really interesting. I'd love you to see it. There are all these portraits—"

"It's all right," said Tom nobly, "honestly."

"Well," she said doubtfully, "if you're sure. I suppose we could swap over and you could go in afterwards."

"Here's some money," said Tom's dad, "in case you want an ice cream or something. Be careful with Sophie, won't you?"

"Course we will," said Ash cheerfully. "You'll be all right with us, Sophie, won't you?" And Sophie smiled her uneven smile.

They pushed the chair round the side of the house. Beyond the formal beds, smooth grassy slopes led towards a lake. Ash's eyes lit up.

"Right," he said. "Have you got your seat belt on, Soph? Here we go! Vroom VROOM!" He broke into a run, and soon the wheelchair was hurtling across the grass and Sophie was chuckling with delight. Tom, taken by surprise, stood watching for a moment as the chair careered round in crazy zigzags, and then took off after it.

"I say!" The outraged shout came from a smart elderly lady who had just come out of the shop. "Is that one of our chairs? What on earth do you think you're doing? Have you no respect for anything? They're for people who can't walk – they're not to play with!"

They stopped. Ash went red. "What's it to do with you?" he said angrily. The woman opened her mouth to reply, but Tom interrupted smoothly.

"Actually," he said, "it doesn't belong to you. It belongs to my sister, and she can't walk because she had a stroke. That's why she needs it. My parents are inside the house. You can check with them if you want to. We couldn't go in with them – because of the wheelchair. Because you don't seem to have access for the disabled."

The woman looked embarrassed, and Tom felt delight in the power words had given him. "Oh. Oh, I see. Well – that's all right then, I suppose." And she carried on, rather quickly, into the house.

"Nice one!" said Ash. "Silly cow. I was going to have a go at her. But you sorted her out all right. Did you see her face?"

They went all the way round the lake, taking it in turns to push Sophie's wheelchair and running with it till they had no breath left. Then they sat down on a bench looking over the lake. Ducks paddled pompously and swans sailed serenely. The sun was warm; pale lemony primroses speckled the grass.

"Tell you what," said Ash to Sophie. "Do you want to see if you can get out of that chair?"

"Can," she informed him.

"Can you?" He looked at her, considering. "Nah. Don't believe you."

"Can!" she snapped, and leaned forward.

"Just a minute!" said Ash, and he moved the footrests out of the way. Then he held out his hands. He took hold of Sophie's right arm, clasping it firmly underneath her elbow, and she held on to his other hand with her left one.

Tom was anxious. What if she fell? "Careful!" he warned. "I'm not sure you should do that!"

But they were both concentrating fiercely and didn't seem to hear him. Slowly, very slowly, her eyes fixed on Ash's, Sophie uncurled her body and eased her way upright.

"Brilliant!" enthused Ash. "Now, I'm going to step back. Nice and slow, don't worry. Move that foot first." He pointed with his foot to her left one. She moved it forward. "Then the other one."

Sophie was frowning. Tom felt sure she couldn't do it. He could tell she was trying really hard, but nothing was happening. Then she seemed to take all her weight on her left leg, and swung her right one from the hip. It looked odd, but it worked. Her frown disappeared, and her face glowed with pleasure.

"Sophie! What—" The cry tore a hole in their concentration. As Mum, swiftly followed by Dad, came running across the grass, Sophie turned to look, lost her balance and collapsed awkwardly back into the chair.

"What on earth do you think you're doing?" Mum looked terrified and angry at the same time. "She's not ready for that yet!"

"Ash!" Sophie stretched out her left hand imperiously. "Again!"

"No!" cried Mum. But Dad put out a hand and touched her arm.

"Wait," he said. "Just look at her face. Now what's wrong with that?"

Mum looked. Sophie's face was eager. Ash's was anxious. Then Mum said reluctantly, "All right. Go on then – try it again!"

Tom watched. There was a spellbound circle. Inside it were Mum – smiling now – Dad, Sophie and Ash. But he was on the outside, watching. Why hadn't he been the one who'd thought to help Sophie stand? Why couldn't he have been the hero?

Sophie was so tired. She'd enjoyed the day, but she was glad that they were on their way home so she could just let herself sink into sleep. Everything she did was hard – every single thing. Nobody seemed to understand that. They nagged her about using both hands, when it was so much easier to manage with one. They nagged her about doing exercises, when, so far as she could see, they were making no difference. They made her see a procession of experts, each of whom seemed to be interested in a different part of her. The other day it had been a speech therapist. She'd been all neat and buttoned up, with shiny hair and a prissy, tinkling voice. She'd wanted Sophie to look at pictures and tell her what they were, as if it wasn't obvious. What kind of an idiot did she take her for? The voice inside Sophie had screamed at her, but she couldn't find the words she needed. If she'd been able to she would have walked out, but that wasn't an option, so she had simply shut down and blanked the speech therapist out.

She would do just as much she needed to do. It took a huge amount of effort – no one knew how much. She didn't have the energy to do more. The first thing she had to do was learn to walk again. Mum and Dad wanted her to do other things, she knew that. They wanted her to smile and talk to them, and show them that she was all right, that she was happy. Well, she'd do all that one day. But not now. Because for now, she needed every bit of strength she had to focus on making her body work for her again. There was nothing to spare, nothing extra.

She closed her eyes and relaxed into sleep.

She woke up when they were nearly home. The

Willow Man bowed, congratulating her. No one else saw. They didn't see much at all really. *He* knew how hard it was. In her mind, she spoke to him. "I'll be free. Oh, yes I will! And when I am, you will be too..." Why did they think they could hold him there? He wasn't made of something dead, like stone or bronze, he was made of living willow. He was magic and so was she. She blew him a kiss.

"Is Sophie awake?" asked her mother.

"Ow! Yes, she's trying to poke my eye out," grumbled Tom.

Poor Tom. She hadn't meant to hurt him. She leaned her head against his arm. After a moment he patted it awkwardly.

First Steps

After Saturday, Tom's mum and dad seemed to have decided that Ash was a good thing, and he came round often. He wasn't just Tom's friend any more – he was everyone's friend. Tom wasn't sure what he thought about this. He had been angry when his mother had seemed doubtful about Ash, but now that she'd changed her mind he felt annoyed all over again. It's only because of Sophie, he thought. Ash can get Sophie to do things and that's why Mum likes him. Everything's to do with Sophie now. Everything.

Since Ash had helped her take that first step, it seemed there was no stopping her. The next Friday, when they came home, Mum told them how Sophie had walked all by herself.

"No one was watching her. There was a little party for Steven – he was the boy who'd been in that terrible car accident, do you remember? He's been in hospital for months, and he was going home, so the nurses did sandwiches and biscuits and things. We were all down that end of the ward, and I just glanced up to see if Sophie was OK, and there she was, on her feet, out of her chair, tottering down the ward. I think we must have been shocked or something, because none of us could move. We were all terrified – she looked so unsteady, we thought she was bound to fall down. But she didn't. It was amazing!"

"I wish I'd seen it," said Dad. Mum looked at him.

"Poor you," she said. "You miss everything, don't you? Like when they were little, and they took their first steps while you were at work."

"Not everything," said Dad, looking a bit annoyed. "I saw Tom's first step. In fact, I think it was you who missed that. You'd gone shopping, and it was just me and Tom."

Tom felt oddly pleased. One up for us, he thought.

"Oh. Well, anyway, you won't miss much more, because they're so pleased with how she's getting on that they say she can come home."

Dad looked puzzled. "But what about all the physio she needs? How will she get that?"

"She'll have physios who'll come and see her at home, I think. Or maybe I'll have to take her to see them. I'm not sure yet."

"Oh. And what about school?"

"They think it'll be good for her to start back as soon as possible. Only part-time, of course. But that means I'll be able to go back to work, which is just as well – the council have been really good, but I can't expect them to keep my job open for ever."

"But do you think we'll be able to manage if you go back to work? I won't be able to have time off school, so the ferrying about will be down to you. Will you be able to fit it all in?"

She frowned. "Well, I'll just have to, won't I? Somehow or other."

"Yes, but the most important thing is—"

"I *know* what the most important thing is! Do you seriously think you need to tell me?"

Tom wasn't used to hearing his parents arguing. He felt uncomfortable. Dad glanced at him. "Well, we don't need to worry about it just now, do we? It'll be great to have Sophie home all the time, Tom, won't it? And Mum."

Tom mumbled something and said he had to do some homework.

"On a Friday?" said Mum, startled.

"Might as well," he said, and made his escape up to his room. He saw that Sophie's light was still on: she never went to sleep in the dark. On impulse, wondering if she'd heard the raised voices, he pushed the door open quietly. She lay among her cushions; at first she'd needed them to keep her propped up, but now they just seemed to belong there, like Beethoven. Her curtains were open and she was gazing out at the rectangle of dark blue, star-scattered sky.

She must miss the television, he thought. On the ward she'd had one beside her bed all the time. He had an idea. "Do you want to listen to a tape, Soph? A story tape?" She nodded.

He went into his own room and rummaged about till he found the shoebox with his old tapes. He found a *Just William* one and grinned. She'd enjoy that, it was really funny. He took it into Sophie's room and put it on her cassette player.

"You'll like this," he promised.

As he left, he noticed Ash's drawing of the Willow Man. It was on Sophie's desk, at the bottom of the bed.

"What do you reckon, Soph?" he said. "Is he waving or dancing?"

Sophie shook her head, smiling. "Not dancing," she said. "Waving. To me." Tom looked again. There were shadows at the edge of the room and it was difficult to see clearly.

"Yes," he said doubtfully, "of course he is."

He went back to his own room and put a CD on. But quietly, so as not to disturb Sophie.

Reading

The next day, Ash was going round to see Tom. Matthew was already up when he came downstairs.

"Can I play with your Lego, Ash? Will you show me how to make dinosaurs?"

Ash hesitated. He hadn't played with his Lego for ages, but it was still there in a box under his bed. Some of the dinosaurs he'd made were still on his shelf, and he had promised that one day he'd show Matthew how to make them.

"Sorry, Matt, I can't. I'm going round to Tom's."

Matthew scowled. "You're always going round there!"

His mother came in, carrying the post.

"What's wrong with that?" she said to Matthew. "Tom's Ash's friend. And Kieran's your friend, and he's coming round later to play. So that's OK, isn't it?"

Matthew still looked sulky. "I want to play with the Lego. Ash said I could. He said he'd show me."

"And I will," promised Ash. "I'll show you later, when I come back. All right?"

As he ate his cornflakes, his mother glanced through the pile of envelopes and leaflets.

"All junk, as usual," she said. "Oh – hold on – a real letter! Now, who on earth...?"

After a couple of minutes, when she hadn't said anything, he glanced up. She was staring at the letter in her hand. She seemed transfixed.

"What's up?" he said. "Is it something bad?"

She pushed it back into the envelope hastily. "No, no! It's just – a bill. That's all it is. Nothing that matters. Nothing at all. Can you just take Harry out before you go?" She stood up abruptly and went upstairs.

Later on, when he got round to Tom's, Ash mentioned the letter to him.

"It was odd," he said thoughtfully. "She said it was a bill, but it wasn't – she'd already said it was a letter. And it wasn't in a brown envelope. She seemed really upset."

"Ash! Ash!" It was Sophie's voice.

"Well, *she* sounds cheerful anyway!" said Ash. He went into the living room. Sophie was standing, holding onto the back of an armchair.

"Watch!" she commanded.

And she walked. She was lopsided and tottering, but she walked. She went across the room, leaning further and further forward as she went, then collapsed onto the settee and lay there giggling.

"Brilliant!" grinned Ash. "And you did it all by yourself, alone! What a star!"

So then she had to do it again, and they clapped and marvelled – well, Ash did, and Tom halfheartedly copied him – and then Dad came in to see what all the noise was about, so she showed him too, and he hugged her.

"No," said Sophie severely, and she put both arms round his waist, so that *she* was the one doing the hugging. Dad looked puzzled, but by then Mum had come in as well, and she explained.

"Sophie's new occupational therapist, Helen, went into school this week to see how things are going. She seems really nice. She was explaining to the teachers how important it was to find things for Sophie to do that'll make her use her right arm – like cleaning the whiteboard. Wasn't she, Sophie?"

Sophie nodded seriously.

"And she's not to try to write or anything with her left one, because if she does, it'll just take over and the right one won't have a chance. So she has to use both arms to hug her teacher. It's sort of an exercise," said Mum.

"Ah," said Dad. "So the teachers get lots of lovely hugs, do they?"

"Yes," said Mum, looking a bit envious, "They do. Sophie seems to enjoy doing that. Anyway, we'd better get on." She turned to Tom and Ash. "Would you two mind looking after Sophie, just while we take Dad's car to the garage for a service? I need to go with him to give him a lift back."

Tom had been planning to show Ash his new computer game – Ash didn't have a computer at home. He sighed.

"All right," he said. "What should we do with her?"

"You make her sound like a parcel," said Mum, going through to the kitchen. "You could play a game. Or – I tell you what would be really useful. You could find some of her old books and see if you can get her to do some reading."

"But she reads to herself," objected Tom.

"Not any more, she doesn't. I thought at first it was because it was difficult for her to hold a book, but I don't think it's just that. She won't read even if I'm holding the book. Maybe she will for you." She looked a bit sad for a moment, the same as she'd looked when she was talking about Sophie hugging the teacher.

"All right," he said unenthusiastically. He could see that Ash wasn't too keen either.

"I'll go and look out some of her books," said Mum, "and then we'll be off. We won't be long."

But when Tom showed the books to Sophie, she shook her head. "Don't want to," she said.

"Go on. Just have a go," he urged. "Please?"

Tom picked one out.

"You read it," said Sophie to Ash. He looked embarrassed.

"No," he said.

"Please!" she said.

"No – you!"

She shook her head again. "You."

Tom looked at Ash. "Oh, go on. Anything for a quiet life."

"No. No, I—"

Sophie picked the book up, and held it out to him. She had it in her left hand, but she carefully reached her right one out, and pushed it underneath the book. Ash stared, but Tom suddenly realized what she meant.

"She means she's doing *her* bit, because she's using both hands – and you've got to do your bit. That's reading to her."

"All right, then," said Ash, turning back to Sophie. "You read and I'll listen. How about that?"

Sophie thought about this, then nodded. Ash smiled, but he looked uncomfortable. He sat down beside her on the settee, balancing on the edge as if all he wanted to do was run away.

Sophie began to read. After a few words she hesitated. She read one or two more and then she stopped, her expression puzzled.

"Come on," said Ash, "you can do it, I bet you can!"

But Sophie shook her head.

Ash pointed. "This is where you are. What's it say? Just have a go, go on!"

Another silence. Tom felt impatient. It was obvious it wasn't working – couldn't Ash see that? "It'll take ages like that. You might as well just tell her if she's stuck. Look, Soph – 'dungeon,'" he said. " 'The castle had a dungeon.' Now you do the next line."

Sophie read a little further, then stopped, looking at Ash. Tom caught the glance and moved away. "Go on then, you carry on," he told Ash.

"No, no, that's all right," said Ash hastily. "You do it. You're much better at it."

After a few words, she seemed to lose interest. Ash was staring at the floor, his face glum. Tom looked from one to the other, trying to sense what to do. There was something difficult in the atmosphere, something he didn't understand. Why were they both so grumpy? It wasn't such a big deal, surely? Puzzled, he suggested that they should go for a walk.

"We can push you, Soph, like last week at Wivenhoe House."

But it wasn't at all like last week. Then, Ash's mood had lifted them. Now, it wrapped itself round them like a damp fog. They were all silent for a while, but finally Ash spoke.

"What it is," he said, looking carefully down at his feet, "is reading."

"What do you mean?" asked Tom, not understanding. "What about reading?"

"Can't do it," said Ash gruffly.

Tom couldn't get the hang of this at all. "Can't do what?"

Ash glared at him. "Read! I can't read!"

"You what? How do you mean? Of course you can read – you must be able to!"

"Oh, is that right? Well, I can't. Not properly, anyway. I can read some of the words, but they – I dunno, they kind of jump about, and I – oh, never mind!"

Sophie was gazing up at him, her face troubled. Ash looked at her.

"Even after what's happened to Sophie, she can read better than me. I'm – I'm just stupid. That's it. That's what it is."

He unclenched his hands, moving them in front of him as if he was trying to contain something within them. Then he said to Tom fiercely, "You're not to say anything to anybody. Not your mum and dad, not teachers, not anybody. Right?"

"No," said Tom, bewildered. "Of course I won't."

"Good!" scowled Ash. Then he turned and set off back towards Bridgwater, his shoulders hunched as if against a storm.

A Bargain

Ash was angry. The anger crackled around him like little tongues of flame; Sophie could almost see it. Tom was staring after him; he seemed to have forgotten she was there. She felt impatient. If only she could explain! It was so obvious to her – Ash needed their help. He had helped her. She hadn't wanted to do anything – she'd been so sick of everyone going on at her. But somehow Ash had made starting to walk again fun. He'd made her want to do it, and once she'd managed the first few steps the next ones and the ones after that had seemed much easier.

And she knew they could do the same for him. She wasn't exactly sure how it would work, but she did know what the first step would be. But it wasn't easy – to take it she would need Tom's help. She couldn't do it by herself.

Awkwardly, she turned in the chair and reached

up to touch his arm. He looked down at her.

"What?" he said. He thought she was a nuisance. That didn't matter. She'd often thought the same about him. And he thought she was interfering, because Ash was his friend, not hers. That didn't matter either. What mattered was that she must make him understand.

She concentrated hard on what she needed to say. Talking was much easier now than it had been to start with, after the thing had happened. It was slow, but she could say what she needed to. It was just that often it was easier to say nothing at all and just let everything happen in front of her, like a video that she could watch but not be a part of.

"The Willow Man," she said carefully. "We should go to him."

"Why?" Tom was bewildered. "Don't you think we should go after Ash?" He looked again towards Ash's figure, tiny now in the distance.

She shook her head earnestly. "No," she said. "The Willow Man can help Ash."

He stared at her. "How?"

"He will," said Sophie firmly. "He can."

He didn't believe her. She could see it in his expression, troubled and undecided.

She gripped his wrist. Her left hand was very strong, now that it had to do the work of two.

"Ouch!" he cried. "Stop it! That really hurts!"

She released him and then gazed at him steadily. "Please," she said. *"Please!"*

It took longer than she'd expected for Tom to push her to the fence round the field where the Willow Man lived. Tom was quiet, and she could feel his crossness. It wasn't as powerful as Ash's anger: brownish grey rather than flaring red. Perhaps the Man could help him too.

"Now what?" demanded Tom. "Do you expect me to get the chair over the fence?"

She sighed. Boys could be so stupid, especially brothers. She inched forward in the chair, getting ready to stand up.

Tom was gazing absently at the Willow Man. The sun was behind the figure's arm, but then something odd happened: the arm seemed to move, as if it was beckoning, releasing the sun, so that its rays reached out and dazzled Tom. Sophie was urging him to help her. Confused, he did, letting her lean on him, helping her lift her right arm and foot, almost carrying her over the fence. They leaned against it, breathless. But it was a large field and the figure still seemed a long way off.

"You can't go all that way, Soph," he said, knowing that that was where she wanted to be. She grinned at him and launched into her unsteady walk. "No!" he said. "Don't be stupid; it's too far, you'll fall!" She took no notice. Trying not to think about what his mother would say and furious with Sophie for being so stubborn, he went after her. She put her left arm through his right one so that she could lean on him, and slowly they stumbled across the field.

Around the figure's feet the grass was long, and there were flowers.

"Pick some," ordered Sophie. Her eyes were fixed on him, trying to explain what she couldn't find the words to say.

"*What?*"

She looked at him as if he was very silly, knelt down awkwardly, and showed him what to do.

"I know what you want me to do," he said, irritated. "I just don't know why."

Sophie gestured towards the Willow Man. "For him," she said simply.

"But—"

"And for Ash."

The field was low-lying and damp. He found some flowers that he didn't recognize, with slender stems that carried a crown of pale lilac blossoms. There were some long grasses that seemed quite pretty, so he added a few of those too.

Sophie was looking pale and tired now, but she had picked some that were near her. She tried to tie them all together with a piece of grass, but it was too difficult with only one hand. She looked angry, and for a moment Tom thought she was going to crush them like she had the irises at home. But she didn't, and he tried to do what she wanted.

"There," he said. "Now what?"

She held up her arms for him to help her up. Then she took the bunch of flowers and said, "Close your eyes. Wish…"

He thought he had closed his eyes, but he could see the sunlight through his eyelids, and then he must have opened them a tiny crack. Or maybe he just thought he had, because he wasn't sure what he'd seen, or, really, if he'd seen anything. Well, he couldn't have. He might have seen Sophie hold up the flowers, but he couldn't possibly have seen the Willow Man bend gracefully down and take them. It must have been something to do with the sunlight again – when you stared into the sun with your eyes closed, it *did* make funny patterns on the inside of your eyelids…

They managed to get back across the field and over the fence, and Sophie sighed with relief as she settled back into the chair.

When they got back to the house Mum and Dad were back from the garage.

"You've been out for a walk," said Mum, stating

the blindingly obvious, as she often did. "But where's Ash?"

"Um…" began Tom, when he was saved by a knock at the door. It was Ash.

"He's here," said Tom brightly. "He – er – had to go and get something. From the shop. Come on up, Ash, I'll show you that computer game."

"Sorry," said Ash, once they were out of earshot.

"What for?" asked Tom.

"For getting mad. For going off. Stupid. It's just – it's just—"

"Don't worry about it," said Tom hastily. "Just forget it. Come on, have a go at this game."

But a little later, when they went down for something to eat, Tom's mum waylaid them.

"How did you get on with the reading?" she asked them conspiratorially, checking that Sophie was in the living room and couldn't hear. "Any good?"

"Not brilliant," said Tom. "It was like you said. She read a little bit and then she'd had enough."

"Oh." She looked disappointed. "Well, thanks for trying."

"It wasn't me," said Tom. "She wanted Ash to read to her."

"It's funny how she'll do stuff for some people and not for others," said his mum thoughtfully.

"Ash – she really does seem to have taken to you. Perhaps it's because you make it all seem like fun. I wonder… I know it's a pain, but I wonder if you would have another go with her?"

Ash looked horrified.

"Oh," said Tom's mum, surprised. "Well, of course, if you really don't want to…"

Ash found his voice. "No – I didn't mean—"

"Oh, good," she said, sounding relieved. "It was just that for a minute you looked really unhappy about the idea, and I wouldn't want to push you into anything. But I really think it might help. Did you leave the books out, Tom?"

Tom suddenly had a thought. "Yes," he said "they're still there. But I was thinking: perhaps it would be better for Sophie if we used some easier books. Have we still got any of our old picture books?"

"What a good idea! Hang on – I'll go find some. I know exactly where they are…" In a few minutes she was back. "There you are, Ash – have a go with these. And Tom, you could take them some drinks and biscuits."

A little later, Tom went through to the sitting room, dreading the awkward silence that had invaded the room earlier.

But it wasn't there. Ash's spiky brown head and Sophie's wavy blonde one were bent over a book about bears. Ash was reading a line slowly. Then Sophie did the same. When she'd done her bit, she looked up and beamed at Tom. She looked extremely pleased with herself.

Tom grinned back. There was no need for him. But this time, he didn't mind. He'd fixed it. The picture books had done the trick. It wasn't just Ash who had good ideas – it was him too. He went up to his room, put a CD on, and lay on his bed. The sun was shining through the big silver birch in the garden, and the wind made the branches dance so that dappled specks of sunlight rippled and swayed on the carpet. He felt calm. No, not just calm – he actually felt happy!

Team Weaving

Over the next few days, Tom thought a good deal about Ash not being able to read properly. What he couldn't work out was how no one had noticed. He set himself to track how many times in a day he needed to be able to read, and to try and work out how he would manage if he couldn't. He began at breakfast on Monday morning.

The first thing was the cereal packet. Tom often positioned the Shreddies or Bran Flakes packet in front of him while he ate his breakfast and read through the stuff written on the packet. He did it partly to give his eyes something to do while his brain carried on sleeping and partly to avoid having to talk to anyone.

But it wouldn't really matter if he couldn't do that. You didn't need to be able to read to know what was in the packet, because of the picture on the front. So that wouldn't be a problem. Anyway,

Ash could read a bit – he must be able to, or else he wouldn't have been able to read any of the words in the bears book.

What about school, though? That was the big one. How was it possible that no one at school had noticed that Ash was so bad at reading? He decided to watch carefully in class to see how Ash managed to get by.

The first lesson was maths. That didn't seem to be too much of a problem. Ash's work was untidy, but he seemed to find geometry easier than Tom did. Then it was art, and of course that was fine – he was good at art. But after break it would be English, and surely he would have to be able to read for English?

But actually, he didn't. They didn't often read books in class, and even when they did, Miss Palmer either read the book herself or gave them chunks to read at home. And of course it was well-known that Ash and homework didn't mix – that was one of the main things he got detentions for.

Tom noticed that Ash watched all the teachers very carefully when they were giving instructions. He hardly looked at the board at all. He must be memorizing what they said. The work he came up with wasn't very good, but then again, none of them expected it to be. They thought Ashley was stupid and lazy and disorganized. But after a few days, Tom could see that actually he had to work really hard just to get by. He wasn't lazy or stupid – it just seemed that way if you didn't look very carefully.

It wasn't right. But Ash had said he wasn't to tell anybody about it, and Tom knew he'd meant it. So it looked as if it was all down to Sophie. Ash came round a couple of evenings in the week now. He couldn't usually make it straight after school because of having to pick his little brother up, but he sometimes came later on after tea, when he was taking Harry for a walk. Sophie made it very clear that no one else was allowed in the room while they were reading, so Tom didn't know exactly how well either of them was getting on, but they seemed to be getting through a lot of books – Mum had had to sort out some more for them.

"I really think she's turned a corner," Tom's mum had said one evening to his dad. "It's not just the reading – she seems to be more interested in everything. Much more the old Sophie. Helen's really pleased with her."

Tom had met Helen a couple of times – usually Sophie went to see her, but sometimes she came to the house. She was quite old, probably even a bit older than Mum and Dad, but she was funny and nice. She was the one who'd had the idea about hugging teachers.

"There are people who hug trees, believe it or not," she'd said, "but I bet you're the only person in the world who has to hug teachers!"

Last time she had come to the house, she'd brought a jigsaw puzzle with big chunky pieces.

"This is for you, Tom," she'd said. "Well, sort of. I thought that you could do the puzzle with Sophie. She'd have to use her right hand to pick the pieces up, and that's really hard for her, so you'd have to do something hard too – maybe use your left hand or your toes or something."

Tom remembered the puzzle when his mother mentioned Helen. It was a map of the world, showing the animals that lived in different places, so there was a polar bear prowling across the Arctic, and an upside-down sloth in South America. He hadn't bothered suggesting it to Sophie at the time, because for one thing, he didn't think that she'd be interested, and for another thing, he wasn't either.

But now it struck him that it might be a good idea, and that Ash might like to do it too – after all, it was pictures, not words. They had a great time picking up the pieces between their toes while Sophie pushed them into place. Then he remembered a plastic skittles set at the back of the cupboard in his room, and they had a go with that too. Sophie couldn't throw the ball with her right hand, but she could give it a shove with her fist.

*   *   *

Tom also found that he could help Ash with his homework. He had to be careful about it, though. He sensed that if he offered help outright, Ash would curl up like a hedgehog and present Tom with an unfriendly set of prickles. So he suggested that they should do their homework together – particularly when he knew there was something Ash was likely to have trouble with.

If there was a worksheet, Tom would read it out as they went along. Then he would write an answer, read it out loud and ask Ash what he thought. Ash was good at thinking – it was just reading that seemed to be a problem.

And for one piece of work – a story for English – he helped Ash to do it on the computer. It wasn't very long, but they used the spell check, and messed about with the font and the title and everything so that it looked twenty times better than anything he had handed in before. Miss Palmer looked startled when Ash handed it in.

"Goodness, Ashley Fox," she said, "this looks brilliant! I'm impressed!"

So everything seemed to be going really well. Then, one morning, Ash came into school looking excited.

"Guess what!" he said. "My dad's coming home!"

Barriers

"Coming home? Hey, that's great!" said Tom.

"Isn't it just?" enthused Ash. "I can hardly believe it. It was in that letter – you know, the one I told you about, that Mum got a while ago? I didn't even know they were still in touch – she's never talked about him. I can hardly remember him. He's Irish, but that's about all I know. His family are all in Ireland, that's why we never see them. Well, I suppose it is, anyway. He's called Jack."

As Ash chattered on, Tom began to feel uneasy. He did remember what Ash had said about the letter. He'd said that his mother had been really upset. Why should she have been, if it was good news that his father was coming home? And wasn't it a bit odd that he should be turning up now, after all these years? People were always turning up out of the blue in soap operas, not in real life. But Ash's eyes were shining and gave no hint of doubt.

"There's just a few, like, pictures I can see, of him and me together," Ash was saying. "There was the aircraft museum, where we saw the Harriers. That was only just before he left."

"How old were you then?" asked Tom.

Ash thought. "About six, I suppose. He went soon after Matthew was born. And then there was another time – it must have been a long time before that, because we went up a lot of steps and he carried me on his shoulders. We were high up on a cliff, and it was really windy and I was a bit scared. The sea was a long way below us. It was deep blue, with sparkles on it."

"Couldn't have been anywhere near here, then," said Tom practically, thinking of Weston. "It'd have been mud coloured, not blue." Weston was well known for having tides that took the sea miles away from the shore, so that all you could see was a line of muddy froth in the distance.

"I think it was," said Ash. "I'm not sure, but I think it must have been Brean Down – you know, where we went on that geography field trip last year?"

Tom remembered. It had been very windy, and the sea had been a long, long way down. He felt slightly sick just remembering. He hated heights. He hated deep water too. There was no end to the number of ways he wasn't a hero.

"Too right," he said. "It was really high up, wasn't it?"

Ash glanced at him, not understanding. "Yes, I suppose it was. It was funny, you know. I had the feeling as soon as we got there that I'd been there before – you know how that sometimes happens? And then all of a sudden it clicked, that it was the place I remembered. It's the one place where I can really kind of see my dad. The funny thing is, even there I can't see his face because I was on his shoulders. But I can feel his hair in my fingers … curly it was, and dark. Not straight like mine. And I can remember the feeling." He paused. "I felt safe even though I was so high up. I felt warm and safe. And Mum was there too – we were all together."

"So when's he coming?"

"On Friday. So I won't be able to come round this weekend. I expect we'll be doing stuff together."

Sophie was cross when Tom said that Ash wouldn't be coming round at the weekend. Ash had let her down. And not just her. A promise had been made when she and Tom had given the flowers to the Willow Man. She had given them to him because she sensed his power, just as she sensed his sadness. He was sad because he was stuck. Just as she was, just as Ash was. And maybe Tom, too: she didn't know exactly why Tom was stuck, but she could tell that he was. He looked angry sometimes, and other times he looked sad. And so she had made her request to the Willow Man.

After the stroke, she had allowed a barrier to rise up between her and the world. It felt safer and easier to hide behind. But when Ash had helped her to walk, she'd begun to see that it might be better to come out from behind the barrier. It wouldn't always be difficult: Ash had showed her that it could be fun.

Then he'd told them about the reading. Perhaps it was as hard for him not to be able to read as it was for her not to be able to walk. And she'd seen that she might be able to bring about a balance. He had helped her, and she could help him. But only if he would let her.

And that had been what she'd asked the Willow Man. He had to help Tom and her find a way to help Ash. And he'd taken the flowers – he'd accepted the deal. She had felt his surprised gratitude, and the bargain had been struck. Ash would help her, and she and Tom would help Ash. They each had a part to play, and if they did it well, things would change for all of them.

But Ash hadn't been round all week. Something was going wrong. He was letting them down.

Dad offered to read with her instead of Ash, and she allowed him to, and she listened. But she wouldn't read herself. He tried to trick her into it – he'd suddenly stop reading and say something like, "And what did Susan say then?", and point at the line. But she was never fooled. She would just look at him silently and wait for him to give in and carry on reading. Because it wasn't his job to listen to her reading, it was Ash's.

When Sophie went to bed, she sat propped up among her cushions and gazed at Ash's card of the Willow Man. The drawing was very good. It showed how he was made, with all the strips of willow woven tightly together, giving him strength and form. As she looked she began to feel uneasy. He wasn't made of bronze or concrete, like a statue. If he had been, he wouldn't have been alive; he wouldn't have been special. But perhaps being alive also made him weak. You couldn't destroy bronze or concrete. But you could destroy living willow.

It was a long time before she was able to sleep, and when she did her dreams were troubled by the figure of a man whose face she couldn't see. He moved stealthily and silently, slipping through the streets of Bridgwater and across the fields till he had almost reached the Willow Man. She knew she had to stop him – no one else knew how dangerous he was. But she couldn't move. She was in her wheelchair and there was no one to push her. She got out of the chair and walked as far as she could, but that was nowhere near far enough. Soon she was limping badly. It was too hard; she was exhausted, she couldn't do it alone. She sank to the ground and tried to put her hands over her ears to shut out the scream of fear and pain. But she couldn't lift her right hand far enough. She had no choice but to hear.

The Homecoming

Ash thought they should all go to the bus station to meet his father, but Mum didn't agree.

"It's been a long time," she said shortly. "I'm sorry, Ash, I know you want it to be all happy families, but I don't think it's going to be like that. You stay and look after Matthew. We'll be back soon enough."

Why wouldn't she talk about his dad? Even now, when he was practically on the doorstep? And Matthew was no better. He looked as if he was about to cry.

"Come on," said Ash, "cheer up. What about doing a nice picture for Dad? A welcome home picture?"

Matthew frowned. "He's not my dad," he said. "I haven't got one."

Ash sighed. "I know he's not been here," he said, "but he's going to be now. That's good, isn't it?"

"Where's he been?" challenged Matthew. "Why did he go away? I don't want a dad anyway. *I* don't need one." And he sat down to watch television, knees crossed, arms folded, with a horrible scowl on his face.

Ash gave up and went up to his room to draw. He'd always liked drawing and painting. Lately, all his pictures had been of the same thing. He'd pinned the best ones on the wall. He looked at them. They were all of the Willow Man. In some, he was a distant figure in a big empty landscape. In others, he filled the whole page, looming and dark. In some, the sky was stained an angry red. In others, the light was gentle and sunny. He had an idea and settled on his bed, his sketchbook leaning against his knees.

He had just finished when he heard the sound of the door downstairs and the murmur of voices. He hadn't noticed that time had been passing, and looked at the page in front of him to see what he had drawn. The Willow Man was no longer alone. He had a Willow Wife, and two Willow Children. He grinned. It was silly, he knew. A child's dream. All the same ... he touched the picture as if it had some magical ability to grant a wish.

A few drops of rain splattered on the window pane and the wind sighed round the house. The smile died on Ash's face. He hadn't realized that he'd missed having a father until there was suddenly the prospect that the space might be filled.

As he'd told Tom, he couldn't remember much about his father. He couldn't clearly remember his leaving, not the way he could remember that day on Brean Down. It was all a bit jumbled, really. Matthew had suddenly been there, a tiny new brother, and just as suddenly his father had gone. And since then no word – nothing. It had been only the three of them: Ash, Mum and Matthew. And they'd managed fine, for the most part. Especially since Mum got her job. School hadn't always gone particularly well, and sometimes he'd looked with envy on friends who seemed to have a great safety net of grandparents, aunts and uncles – especially at Easter and Christmas. He'd have liked more Easter eggs and presents. But apart from minor details like that, they'd been all right.

Only lately, spending time with Tom and his family had made him think a bit. It had been fun going off for the day, all together – even if it was just to see some mouldy old house. He could see that the Sophie thing had been difficult for them, but he could also see that it helped having more people to cope with it. If he or Matthew were ever seriously ill, how would they ever manage? Mum would lose her job for a start, he was sure of that. The supermarket wouldn't let her take all that time off and still keep her job open. And how would they have managed to get up to the hospital for visiting?

No, there was no doubt about it. It would be much more practical to have a father around. Besides, then Ash would have someone to watch football with, the same as he knew Tom and his dad often watched rugby and stuff together.

But he didn't think his mother realized all this. She didn't seem very thrilled about his father coming home. That was worrying. But still, he was sure she'd get over it. Probably it was just the shock.

He heard the door opening downstairs. They were back. It was time to meet his father.

The living room seemed very full even though there was only one more person than usual. Ash stood in the doorway for a moment to take in what was happening. Matthew was still curled up on the settee. His mother was just bending down to switch the television off. And the man who must be his father was standing in the middle of the room, looking lost. There was a big holdall at his feet. He wasn't as tall as Ash had expected, and his hair was cut very short, so there weren't the curls Ash remembered.

Ash moved forwards, and his father must have heard him because he turned round.

"Ashley!" he said, with a smile that made his blue eyes gleam with delight. "Look at the fine lad you've turned out to be!" Neither he nor Ash seemed sure of what to do next, but then his father stuck out his hand. "I'm Jack – your father. Put it there, son!" he said. "It's a very great pleasure to see you after all these years."

"Yes, it has been a while," his mother muttered acidly. "Put your bag behind the settee, Jack. You'll be sleeping down here. We don't have a spare bedroom."

Ash thought this was a bit mean. "Matthew could sleep in my room," he suggested, "and – Dad – could have Matthew's."

"Couldn't!" snapped Matthew. "Don't want to, so there!"

"Now, now," said his father hastily, "I wouldn't dream of upsetting anyone. The settee will do just fine. It'll be a sight better than what I've been used to."

Ash wondered what he *had* been used to. Years ago he used to wonder why his father had gone, and where to. He'd imagined that maybe he'd been kidnapped or gone off on some heroic mission to the other side of the world. He'd long since stopped believing that – but where *had* he been? What had stopped him staying in touch?

Uneasily, he pushed the thought away. There'd be time enough for questions and answers. The important thing was that he was here now.

His mother was speaking again. "Well, I can

believe that," she said. Why did she have to use that voice? It was sharp and snippy – not like the way she usually spoke. And Matthew was even worse. He scrambled off the settee with a face as black as thunder and announced that he was going to bed. His father looked disappointed.

"Right you are then, young'un," he said, reaching over to ruffle Matthew's hair. "See you in the morning." Matthew ducked.

"Matthew," he said loudly. "My name's Matthew. Not young'un."

"Oh, sure, of course, Matthew." His father looked at Ash and winked, man to man.

"Would you like a cup of tea?" offered Ash.

"That would be fine, very nice, indeed – unless – you don't happen to have anything a little stronger, do you?"

At a loss, Ash glanced at his mum.

"No, we don't," she said firmly. "It doesn't run to that."

"Oh. Right. No problem at all, then – tea would be just great. Good and strong, with two sugars."

By the time Ash came back with the tea, his mother had fetched a pillow and sleeping bag.

"There you are," she said, dropping them on the floor. "I expect you're tired. I know I am. Is there anything else you need?"

"No," said his father, looking woebegone, "I

don't need a lot. I'm used to managing with not very much at all. Don't you worry about me."

His mother didn't look sympathetic. "I won't. Well, goodnight then." She paused in the doorway. "Come on, Ash, you too. It's late."

It wasn't that late. Ash was going to point this out, but when he saw her face he thought better of it. "Goodnight," he said to his father shyly.

His father smiled. "Thanks for the tea, Ashley. I might just take a look at the television before I turn in." As Ash closed the door behind him, he saw that his father was stretched out comfortably. He looked quite at home.

The next morning, Jack Fox had already gone out when Ash went downstairs. He felt disappointed.

"I didn't think he'd have gone out already," he said to his mother.

She didn't seem to be in any better mood than the night before. "Well, he's used to getting up early where he's been," she observed.

"Where *has* he been?" asked Ash, exasperated.

She looked at him. "Ask him," she said shortly.

But Jack didn't come back till halfway through the afternoon, and when he did he smelt of smoke and beer. He was breezy and cheerful, and when Ash sat down with him he fished a can of lager out of each coat pocket.

"What do you say, Ash? An afternoon in front of the telly watching sport? I expect you have Sky, now?"

"No," said Ash apologetically, "we don't. But – would you like to come and take Harry for a walk?"

"A walk? Well, maybe later. To tell the truth, I'm feeling a bit tired – maybe I'll just have forty winks first." He grimaced. "Just between me and you, that settee wasn't any too comfortable."

Ash felt disappointed. He'd hoped they could have a talk. Still, there was plenty of time – it didn't all have to happen at once.

"Do you want to have a lie-down on my bed?" he offered.

Jack considered. The blue eyes – like Ash's own, he realized – danced mischievously. "Do you think that would be all right with your mother?" he demanded. "I wouldn't like to be in any more trouble with her, and that's for sure."

"It's my room," said Ash. "My bed."

"Well, then. If it's all right with you, that sounds a great idea to me."

His mother and Matthew had been out to the shops. When they returned, she looked round for Jack.

"He's upstairs," said Ash, a little defiantly. "He

didn't sleep very well last night, so he's having a rest on my bed."

She shrugged. "Right. Well, then – have you spoken to him?"

"No. Not yet."

Her glance rested on the two cans of lager and she sniffed. "Oh, I see. No change there, then."

Ash felt bewildered. How were they ever going to be a family again if she carried on being like this?

Jack still hadn't appeared by half past six, and Mum sent Ash up to tell him tea was ready. The room was dark and Ash put the lamp on. His father still didn't wake up. He was snoring softly. Ash wasn't sure what to do. He touched him gently. Nothing. Then he shook his shoulder. Still nothing. He tried again, harder.

This time the result was dramatic. Jack rolled over and sat up in one quick movement. He was tensed, glaring, fierce. Then the staring blue eyes softened as they focused on Ash, and the tension drained out of him.

"Oh. Sorry. I kind of forgot where I was."

"'S all right," said Ash. He felt a bit shaken. For a moment, he had felt really frightened. "Tea's ready," he said, and backed out.

After tea, his father went out for the rest of the evening. Once again, Ash felt disappointed. This wasn't how he'd expected it to be.

But the next morning was different. Ash woke up to find the sun streaming in and his father standing by his bed with a cup of tea in his hand. He put it down, and said cheerfully, "Come on, shake a leg. It's a glorious day and we should be enjoying it! Get your clothes on and we'll be off out."

Matthew wouldn't come – he would still have nothing to do with Jack. But Harry had no such reservations – he seemed to regard Jack as a long-lost friend, frisking happily around him as they walked.

"Dogs always like me," said Jack. "It's just a pity that sometimes people don't," he added with a rue-ful grin, jerking his head back towards the house.

Ash felt a bit uncomfortable about that. Both of them – his mother and his father – seemed to want him to take sides. But he didn't want to have to be on anybody's side – surely it shouldn't be like that?

"Where shall we go, then?" asked Jack. "You'll have to lead the way. As far as I remember, it's not your ideal dog-walking country hereabouts."

"It's all right once you get past the houses," said Ash. He hesitated, and then said, "Sometimes, I go to the field where the Willow Man is."

"The Willow Man? What's that?" asked his father, striding out briskly. Ash explained and Jack listened.

"Oh – is that what all those pictures were of in your room?"

"Yes," said Ash shyly, "yes, that's right." He wondered if Jack had liked them. Tom's mother had said something nice about the card he'd made for Sophie. She'd told him he was good at drawing. He thought about Sophie with a twinge of guilt. He hadn't seen her for a while, what with all the excitement. He wondered if she was reading with someone else now.

But his father was saying something. "So what's the fascination, then?"

"Oh, you'll see when we get there."

When they arrived at the field they leaned on the gate.

"Hm," said Jack. "Well, it's big all right, I'll certainly give you that. All made of willow, you say?" He laughed. "It'd make a fine bonfire, wouldn't it?" He didn't seem very interested – his eyes kept sliding to his watch.

Ash felt oddly let down. He turned away from the figure. He felt as if he'd betrayed someone, but he wasn't quite sure who. Then he stopped and looked into his father's eyes, the eyes which were so like his own.

"Where were you?" he said quietly. "Where were you all those years?"

Jack's eyes fell. "Oh," he said. "I thought your

mother would have told you."

"No. She said I was to ask you."

There was a little silence. Then Jack seemed to come to a decision.

"I've been in prison. That's the truth of it." He darted a glance at Ash, who stood rooted to the spot, stunned. "Not all the time," added Jack hastily. "I wouldn't want you to think that. And not for anything terrible. I was just – unlucky. That's what it was." He paused, and seemed to be thinking. "No, it was more than that. It was bad judgement. But I've paid for it. And it's over. It's important that you should know that." He held Ash's gaze, and Ash began to feel less lost. They walked on.

Ash's thoughts were whirling. Of course. That explained it. Jack hadn't been to see them because he hadn't been able to. But why had his mother never told him? He would have to talk to her. He needed to understand.

He had his chance very soon, because as soon as they got back Jack was off out again. Matthew was at a friend's, so Ash and his mother were alone.

"I suppose that's the last we'll see of him till the pubs close," she said as the door shut behind Jack.

Ash's head felt tight. "Why didn't you ever tell me?" he demanded.

"Tell you what?"

"About Dad. About – where he's been."

She sat down at the kitchen table. "What did he tell you?" she asked.

"That he'd been in prison. Part of the time, not all of it. That he'd been unlucky."

"Unlucky, eh? Not his fault, I suppose."

"He didn't say that." Ash felt angry. Why did she have to twist everything? She wasn't giving his father a chance. So what if he'd been in prison? It didn't mean he was *evil*. He'd done something wrong, he'd paid for it, and now he'd come home. And that was that.

"Why are you *being* like this?" he cried. "He's – he's my father!"

"Yes, more's the pity! It doesn't mean he's welcome here!"

She was still talking, but he couldn't hear her any more because he had his hands over his ears. "Stop it!" he shouted. "Just – stop it!" He ran upstairs to the shelter of his bedroom. It was all going wrong, and it seemed there was nothing – absolutely nothing – he could do about it.

Falling Apart

On Monday, Tom looked out for Ash. He wanted to know what had happened. But all through the morning, Ash chose not to sit with him. He looked upset and pale. He did just what he had to do, and he only spoke if the teachers asked him a direct question. At the end of the morning, Tom waited for him outside the classroom.

"How did it go?" he asked. He felt awkward, because it was obvious what kind of answer it was going to be.

Ash didn't reply straightaway. He kept on walking, his eyes fixed on the ground, heading, as they usually did at lunchtime, for the football field.

"I always wondered why he left," Ash said suddenly. "When I was little I used to think there must be some really good reason. Like he'd been kidnapped or he was a spy and he'd had to go off on a dangerous mission to save the world – you know, stupid stuff like that. Later I thought, well, probably it was just the usual sort of thing – he and Mum weren't getting on, something like that. But that left out why he never got in touch and why Mum would never talk about him."

By this time they were down by the stream that ran along the far side of the field. The grass was dry and they sat down. There was a fence between them and the stream – there wasn't always, but recently fences and gates had been put up all round the school. Tom wasn't sure whether they were there to keep kids in or wild axe murderers out.

Ash was picking daisies and pulling the petals off one by one.

"After a while I didn't think about him that much any more. Just sometimes, I'd imagine what it would be like if he came home. I thought, you know, we'd watch football together on TV. And maybe he'd take me fishing, or we'd all go out at the weekend and fly a kite on the hills. And he'd have a job, so we'd have more money, and Mum wouldn't have to work so hard, and we'd go on holidays."

He was quiet for a while, still picking the daisies. But now he'd begun to split the stems and join them together into a daisy chain.

"But it's not going to be like that," he said flatly. "He's been in prison. That's why he's never been near us. But there's worse. He's my dad. I want

123

him to stay. I thought we'd be a family. But Mum seems to hate him. She won't give him a chance."

He held the daisy chain out to Tom. "Mum showed me how to do this once, a long time ago, when I was little. Give it to Sophie. Tell her I'm sorry I've not been round for a bit."

Tom took it. He had no idea what to say. Once again he felt helpless, an observer of someone else's grief. Ash looked at him despairingly. "I want us to be a family. That's all. Why does it have to be so hard?"

He climbed over the fence and was gone. Tom folded the daisy chain carefully and put it in his pocket. Then he turned and went back into school.

Ash walked. He didn't need to think about where he was going; he cut through the estate, making sure he didn't go near his own house, until he was on the lane that led towards the Willow Man. No one stopped him: he knew how to walk purposefully through the streets as if he had every right to be there.

He sat down with his back against the Willow Man's leg. He closed his eyes and tried to think about nothing.

"Haven't you got any homework?" asked Tom's mum that evening. Sophie was watching television in the sitting room, and, unusually, Tom was sitting at the kitchen table.

"Not sure," said Tom. It was his standard defensive answer; it meant he did know perfectly well, but he wasn't telling.

"Maybe you should go and see," said Mum pointedly.

"Mmm…" said Tom, trying and failing to balance the salt pot on top of the pepper pot.

She sighed. "Or maybe you'd like to set the table?"

"Mum…" said Tom.

"Yes?"

"Do you know Ash's mum?"

She looked at him. "A bit. Not well. You two played once or twice when you were small, and we used to talk in the playground. I thought she was nice. She's had a bit of a hard time, I think."

"Did you know his dad?"

She was stirring onions in the frying pan. She put down the wooden spoon and turned to look at him.

"I never met him. He'd already gone by then, I think."

"But did you know *about* him?"

She picked up the spoon again and began pushing the onions about.

"Why? Why do you want to know?"

"Because he's just come home. And he's been in

prison. Did you know *that*?"

"He's come back?" She dropped the spoon on the floor. "After all these years?"

"Do you know why he was in prison?"

"I think it was for burglary, but I'm not sure. There were lots of rumours. You know – going to prison – it might not have been as bad as it sounds. People go for all sorts of reasons. It doesn't necessarily mean they're bad, or nasty – people make mistakes. But—"

"But Ash's dad is?"

"No, I didn't say that—"

"Ash's dad is what?"

It was Sophie. She didn't need to use the wheelchair inside the house now, and she'd appeared in the doorway, leaning against the frame.

"Come and sit down, Sophie," fussed Mum.

"Is he nasty?" demanded Sophie.

Tom and Mum were both silent. Then Tom remembered the daisy chain. It was in the pocket of his school trousers. Glad to escape, he dashed upstairs to fetch it. It was crumpled and the flower heads had gone floppy, but he gave it to her anyway.

"Ash made it. He asked me to give it to you. He said he was sorry he's not been round," he said, putting it on the table in front of her. She touched it, then picked it up carefully. Saying nothing more, she went out of the kitchen, and they heard her steps dragging up the stairs.

The daisies were dead. The flowers were droopy and brown. Sophie put them in front of the card that Ash had made for her. She felt restless and uneasy. Ash was her friend. He made her laugh. He helped her. And she helped him too, and that was important, really important, because there were a lot of things now that people had do for her – simple things, like cutting up food – and all she could do was be grateful. But Ash needed her help to learn to read. That was their bargain. It was unspoken, but it was real. Since the stroke, it was as if she'd been in a kind of prison. With Ash's help, she'd begun to escape from it. He was in prison too. Not the same kind, and maybe his wasn't as bad; but he still needed to escape from it. And she could help him do it. But if he'd given up, then that was it. If he couldn't keep trying, then why on earth should she?

Who was this father who had appeared out of nowhere? She'd heard what her mother had said about him having been in prison, and she'd seen Tom's face. Something was wrong. She could tell. If Ash had been all right, Tom would have said. But he hadn't.

She felt trapped, caged. She knelt on the bed and pressed her head against the window, trying to see past her own reflection and out into the night. She could feel the Willow Man out there, restless as she was.

"Can't you *do* something?" she pleaded silently. "Can't you help?"

The next day, Sophie's mother took her to the hospital for her weekly session with Helen. Helen was determined to get her to use her right hand. She had explained carefully, several times, that if she tried to use it, really concentrated, it would stimulate her brain to send out the necessary messages to all the nerves and muscles that needed to work together to do even a tiny thing, like picking a pencil up. But if she ignored it, then it wouldn't get any better. Helen wasn't like Rachel at the hospital had been. She understood how difficult it was for Sophie. "It's like a survival instinct," she explained. "Imagine you were a cave man. If one arm's damaged, it's just going to be in your way when you're hunting. So you'll just ignore it, tuck it up out of the way and forget about it. Your body's telling you just to do the best you can with one. But you mustn't take any notice – not if you want to be able to use it again."

Helen got out a game of draughts. It had giant pieces, which made it easier for Sophie's hand to clasp them. Usually she was determined to win, but today she let Helen so that it would finish quicker. Then Helen got her to try and point at things, like the door handle or a chimney through the window. Last week, she had done really well at this, and Helen had got quite excited. But now, her hand felt tight. The fingers curled up and wouldn't open for her. She stared at it. Then she pulled her sleeve down over it, as if to protect it. After a bit, Helen gave up.

"Are you tired, Sophie?" she asked gently.

Sophie shook her head. How could she explain it? For a while it had been fun – her and Ash and Tom, all working together. But now, it was as if Ash had just disappeared. It wasn't fun any more. The exercises just seemed like hard work, and she could see through all of Helen's tricks. Helen looked at Mum, who shrugged.

Then someone had parked behind Mum and it took ages to get the car out. She drove Sophie to school and dropped her in a hurry because she was late for work. Sophie was pale and quiet, and Mrs Bennett looked at her and shook her head. After an hour she rang Mum to say Sophie was too tired for school; they wished they had somewhere for her to rest, but they didn't, so perhaps it would be best if Mrs Healey could come and fetch her. Mum said she'd be there as soon as she could, but they were short staffed in the office, so she'd be a little while.

When she arrived, she hugged Sophie tight and they held on to each other. Then they went home.

Sacrifice

Ash was in school for the rest of the week, but he'd stopped doing homework again and he wasn't even pretending to concentrate in lessons. If he did pick up a pen it was only to draw pictures. Some of the teachers tried getting cross; others just seemed puzzled. Mr Fieldhouse tried to talk to him, but Ash just said politely that everything was fine, and he was sorry he hadn't done his homework, but he'd lost his worksheet, or his book, or his only pen. Big Mac did what he was best at, which was shouting and sarcasm, but Ash just stared at him without reacting.

Then, one morning, he came in with a bruise on the side of his face.

"What happened to you?" asked Tom.

Ash shrugged and said nothing. When Mr Fieldhouse asked him about it, he said he'd banged his head on a shelf. Later, Tom spoke to him again.

"Sophie keeps asking when you're coming round," he said.

"Can't," said Ash. "Not now."

"What's going on?" said Tom, exasperated. "Why won't you talk to me?"

"Am doing. Here we are, look – talking."

"No, we're not. Not properly." Tom hesitated, then said, "That bruise. How did you say you got it?"

"On a shelf."

"You must have had your head in a pretty funny position."

"Oh, it was. Hilarious. It's a laugh a minute in our house. Look, just leave it, right?"

He'd got the bruise the night before. No one had meant it to happen – it just had. Ash had come home to find his father asleep in his room again. It had become a habit: Ash didn't mind. It gave him a chance to be with Jack without his mother's constant watching and listening presence. Ash wished he knew how to persuade her to give Jack a chance, but every time he tried to open the subject, she became all tight-mouthed and sniffy. Ash didn't blame his father for going out to the pub all the time: there wasn't much reason for him to stay at home.

But he did wish Jack wouldn't go out drinking so much. It wasn't that he was horrible when he was drunk – sometimes he could be quite funny – but he wasn't much use as a father like that.

Ash hadn't bothered to wake him up. He'd just switched the lamp on and sat down on the floor with his knees drawn up and his drawing book resting against them. He wondered what he should draw. Usually, lately, he had drawn the Willow Man. In his pictures, the figure had moved. He'd danced and waved and strode far off on mysterious quests. But today Ash felt out of touch. He hesitated, wondering how to start.

Then his father woke up and sat up on the edge of the bed, yawning.

"Ah, that was a fine little snooze! What are you up to, Ash? Homework, is it? No? You need to keep up with your schoolwork, you know – you don't want to end up stupid, like me."

"He won't do that. Not if I have anything to do with it." Mum was in the doorway: they hadn't heard her coming in.

"Mum!" Ash's voice was pleading.

Jack looked at him. "Now, then, Ash, don't look like that, it's all right—"

"No it isn't!" she said angrily. "It's not all right! You can talk – you always could! But you've never been much good for anything else, have you? Where were you when Ash was small? Where were you when Matthew was born? Where you've always

133

been – either in the pub or up to no good! And then you just waltz in, after all these years, and—"

"Stop it!" yelled Ash. "Stop it!" Her words buzzed round in his head like huge, black mechanical bees.

His mother's eyes widened. "Don't you shout at me like that!" She rounded on Jack again. "This is your fault!"

Jack opened his mouth to say something, but Ash had had enough.

"Shut up!" he shouted. "Just – shut up!" He tried to push past his mother, desperate to get out of the room, but there wasn't enough space and he stumbled and somehow hit his face on something. When he sat up, he felt dizzy and his cheeks were wet. He saw Matthew, standing outside the room, his face small and white and scared. His mother tried to help him up, but he pulled away, and then she saw Matthew too, and went to him.

Then he felt his father sitting on the floor beside him. Jack put his arm round Ash's shoulders and hugged him awkwardly.

"Life isn't easy, Ash. Things aren't always as we'd like them to be. It's sad, but true. Your mother's right. I've not treated her well. I've not been much good to any of you..."

Ash buried his head in his arms. He didn't want to hear. He just didn't want to hear.

*　*　*

"How's Ash?" asked Tom's mother the next evening. "It seems like ages since we saw him." Her voice seemed falsely bright, and he looked at her suspiciously.

"He's OK, I think. He wasn't in school today."

"Ah." She didn't sound surprised.

"Why?" he asked. "Have you heard something?"

"Well, yes," she said reluctantly. "I was talking to someone today, someone who lives near Ash. She'd heard that there'd been a row there last night. Those walls are paper thin – everybody knows everybody else's business. I wondered if Ash had said anything to you."

"Well, like I said, he wasn't there today."

She sighed. "Sophie misses him, doesn't she? I'm worried about her."

Tom felt impatient. He'd got used to not worrying about Sophie over the last few weeks. He couldn't cope with being anxious about her as well as Ash; that was just too much.

"Why? She's getting better, isn't she?"

His mother took off her glasses and rubbed her eyes.

"Well, she was. But Helen had a word with me today. She's worried. She says it's as if Sophie's just switched off, like before. It's as if she's gone

135

somewhere, and she won't let us reach her."

Tom went upstairs. Sophie was in her room. He knocked and went in. She had a sketch pad in front of her, and a pencil in her left hand. She was looking at Ash's drawing of the Willow Man, and Tom could see that she'd been trying to copy it.

"That's good," he said. She shrugged and put the pencil down. It wasn't good. She knew it and he knew it. She didn't say anything, but he could see what she was thinking. What was the point of trying?

"Have another go," he said on impulse. "You could draw it for Ash." She looked up at him with a flicker of interest in her eyes. Then she picked up the pencil again and bent over her drawing.

Ash didn't come to school the next day. Tom had Sophie's drawing in an envelope in his bag. He couldn't go home without delivering it, but he didn't know exactly where Ash lived. At registration that afternoon he hung back to talk to Mr Fieldhouse.

"Do you know Ashley Fox's address, sir?" he said. "I just thought I might go round after school and see if he's all right," he added.

Mr Fieldhouse looked at him thoughtfully. "Yes, I do. I suppose it's all right to tell you. It's 68 Avon Way."

"Thanks, sir," said Tom.

"That's all right. And Tom?"

"Sir?"

"Tell him – tell him I hope he'll be back soon. And let me know how you get on. You know—" he looked undecided as to whether he should go on.

"Yes, sir?"

"We have to check up on people who aren't in school pretty quickly these days. If he doesn't come in soon, or if we don't hear from his mother, someone will have to go round there. He's been doing so much better lately – it'd be a shame if it all went wrong."

"Yes, sir. I'll tell him."

Avon Way was easy to find. It was a long road that ran through the middle of the estate. Nervously, Tom knocked at the door of number 68. No one answered. Tom stood back and looked at the windows. One was open upstairs. He knocked again. Still no answer.

Slowly, he turned and went back down the path. As he was walking down the road, he saw Ash coming towards him, holding a little boy by the hand. Ash stared at him, as if he couldn't understand why Tom was there.

"I was just coming to give you this,"explained Tom, holding out the envelope. "Sophie did it for you."

Ash reached for it and drew out the picture.

"Thanks," he said.

Was that it? Tom began to feel annoyed. "It was really hard for her," he said.

"Yes. Well, like I said – thanks."

"You haven't been round for a while. Is everything all right? Aren't you – will you come round soon? Only Sophie won't read except with you. She's – well, she doesn't seem very happy," said Tom feebly.

"No. Sorry. Can't." Ash glanced at the picture, then back at Tom. "Tell Sophie thanks for the drawing." His face looked suddenly angry. "The Willow Man – it's not real, you know. It can't move. It never will move. Nothing changes. I thought it could, but I was wrong." He turned away abruptly, and went up the path. When he'd gone, Tom realized he hadn't passed on Mr Fieldhouse's message. But he didn't think it mattered. He didn't think Ash would have listened.

Sophie's face was eager when he got home.

"I gave it to him," said Tom helplessly. "I did give it to him."

That night, Tom woke up suddenly from a deep sleep. Befuddled, he sat up. There'd been a sharp cry – he realized it had come from Sophie's room. He pushed the duvet back and switched his lamp on. Then the landing light came on, and by the time he reached Sophie's door Mum was already there. Sophie was kneeling on her bed. The curtains were open, and she was staring out of the window. Dad came in next, fastening his dressing gown and rubbing his eyes.

"What's going on?" He yawned.

Before anyone could answer, the night was split by the distant seesawing whine of a fire engine. It grew louder and more urgent. Then the insistent blare filled the room, and the flashing light turned their faces an icy blue as the engine rushed past the house.

Mum was kneeling beside Sophie, paying no attention to the noise. Her eyes were fixed on Sophie's face, desperate and anxious. "Sophie, what is it? Are you all right? Tell me!"

Sophie didn't answer: she seemed frozen. Tom followed her gaze, out into the night. There, in the distance, an orange glow leapt and flickered. For a moment, he didn't understand, and then a blossom of dread began to unfold inside him.

"Oh no," he said. "Oh no."

His mother's voice was angry and uncomprehending.

"What? What are you looking at? *That*? The Willow Man? Is that what this is about? Is that *all*? Do you have any idea how worried I was?

Sophie, I'm talking to you! Answer me, for goodness' sake – just answer me!"

Dad took hold of Mum's hands and spoke to her, trying to soothe her, but Tom didn't listen to what they were saying. Like Sophie, he was mesmerized by the distant flames, which were leaping higher and higher in a fantastic dance. With gathering horror, he saw the tall figure, black against the brilliant background of gold and orange, seeming to twist and writhe as the fire took hold. They watched till the flames, with nothing left to consume, sank lower and lower till they died. The night wrapped its blackness round the place where the Willow Man had been. He was gone. Now he would never be free. It seemed that there was nothing left to hope for.

Aftermath

The next day was awful. They were all exhausted from the night before: Sophie had sobbed and sobbed. Tom had never seen her cry like that, as if her whole body was stricken with hurt and sadness. Mum had held her and eventually lain down beside her, talking softly, smoothing her hair, stroking her face. Dad, looking bemused, had gone downstairs to make some hot chocolate for Tom and him. After a while, Mum came down too.

"She's cried herself to sleep," she said. "Why did it matter so much? Why did she cry like that, Tom?"

Tom shrugged. He couldn't explain to them.

His mother's face was white with tension and worry. "Do you know what I thought?" she asked fiercely. "I thought the stroke was happening all over again. I know that it won't, but all the same, when I heard that cry … and neither you nor Sophie will talk to me, you won't even *try* to explain."

"Leave it, Sarah," said Dad gently. "We're all tired." He looked thoughtful. "I wonder who started it? Someone who'd had too much to drink, I suppose. Or kids, egging each other on."

"*We're* kids," said Tom suddenly. "Why do you think it must have been kids?"

"What? Oh, I don't know. You're quite right, I shouldn't assume that – it could have been any-body. Somebody with a grudge, maybe. Sometimes when people are angry they just want to go out and destroy something. And I suppose if you were looking for something to destroy, the Willow Man would make a very tempting target."

Something came into Tom's mind when his father said that. Something dark and threatening. Something he really didn't want to think about. He got up quickly, put his mug in the sink, said goodnight and went upstairs quietly, so as not to disturb Sophie.

He went to bed and pulled the duvet over his head. But he couldn't shut it out. He couldn't shut out the sound of Ash's voice earlier that day, when he'd said that the Willow Man wasn't real. It wasn't the words so much; it was the feeling that lurked like a shadow behind them. He had sounded angry: betrayed, disillusioned and angry.

Tom woke up with the same feeling he'd had the morning after Sophie had gone into hospital. His father had come home alone the night before. He'd told Tom that they didn't know yet what was wrong with Sophie, but it was all going to be fine, he mustn't worry. Tom had looked into his eyes and known he was lying. Dad didn't *know* that everything was going to be all right.

So Tom hadn't slept that night either – except he must have, because there was that horrible moment when he woke up and knew that the bad thing wasn't just a dream – it was real.

This time, the bad thing was the suspicion that had burrowed into his brain. He was afraid that Ash had made that fire out of his anger and hurt. And if he had, it would be the end of everything that had been getting better – Ash learning to read, Sophie learning to walk again – everything. All of it would stop. Ash would get into terrible trouble and everything would be awful.

He got dressed and went into school as usual. There was a police car parked outside the main entrance. Everyone seemed to know what had happened. Lots of people had been woken either by the fire or by the noise of the engines which had rushed pointlessly along the narrow lane to watch as the Willow Man was reduced to a metal skeleton.

Mr Fieldhouse raised his head and looked round questioningly when he came to Ash's name on the register. When there was no answer he said nothing, but looked grim. Afterwards, he asked Tom if he had seen Ash the day before, as planned. Tom felt himself starting to go red. He wished he was a good liar, but he wasn't. All he could do was try to dodge around the truth.

"Yes," he found himself saying. "Yes, I did see him. He was with his little brother. I think he probably had to stay at home to look after him."

Mr Fieldhouse gazed at him thoughtfully. "You're a very loyal friend, Tom. How did Ashley seem? Was he all right?"

"Yes, sir. Yes, he was fine."

"Really. I'm glad to hear it. Last time he was in school, I didn't think he looked fine at all. Quite the reverse, in fact. Anyway, you'd better get along to assembly."

Mr Fieldhouse was all right, thought Tom. He really sounded as if he was worried. He wondered if he should talk to him about Ash, tell him what he knew.

But after what the head teacher, Mrs Knight, said during assembly, he knew he couldn't possibly talk to anyone at school just in case what he was afraid of turned out to be true.

She spoke about the fire. She said how important

the Willow Man had been. "Make no mistake," she said, "this wasn't like setting fire to some rubbish, or even like burning down a shed. That would be bad enough. But this was far worse. Because the Willow Man was special. When people used to drive past Bridgwater on the motorway, what they noticed was the smell from the cellophane factory. Then the Willow Man was built, and it gave people something different to think about when they thought about Bridgwater – something strong and beautiful and full of energy."

Mrs Knight had metal half-rimmed glasses, and she knew how to use them. She gazed over the top of them now, looking round sternly at everyone in the hall. There wasn't a sound.

"But what will come into the minds of people who drive down the motorway now, as they look at that blackened skeleton? They'll think about the mindless individuals who destroyed it. Is *that* the kind of behaviour we want associated with our town?" Another pause. "Of course it isn't. And it's not the kind of behaviour I want associated with this school. You may have seen the police car outside. The police are determined to find out who did this terrible thing. And they will, you can be sure of that. I hope it doesn't turn out to be anyone from this school. But if it does ..." she said as she whipped the glasses off and directed the full power of her icy blue gaze at them, "... if it does, they will be in more trouble than they can possibly imagine.

"So if any one of you knows anything about it – anything at all – you must not hesitate to speak out. Because if you don't, then you will be to blame too. Make no mistake about that."

As they filed out of the hall, Tom glanced through the glass doors which led into the reception area, to Mrs Knight's office. Mr Fieldhouse was there, and Mr Wilson. They were talking to two policemen.

Mr Fieldhouse was Ash's tutor. Had they somehow put two and two together? Perhaps the police had asked them about likely troublemakers, or about anyone who'd been behaving oddly – perhaps Ash's was the name they had come up with. Tom needed to find Ash. He needed to know the truth.

The corridor was full of people heading towards their first lesson. Tom should have been going towards the science labs. Instead, he went through the double doors and headed past the tennis courts towards the library. Then he took a deep breath and walked quickly out of the back entrance, hoping that if anyone saw him they'd assume he was going to the dentist or something.

He was lucky. No one did see him, and soon he was heading through the estate towards Ash's house.

But he was too late. A police car was in front of him.

It was a long road, with nowhere obvious to hide. He felt like a rabbit caught in headlights. He was in school uniform and it was half past nine. If they saw him, he'd had it. He ducked down behind a parked car. After a few minutes, a woman came past with a pushchair. She looked at him curiously and he took off his shoe and pretended to be looking for a stone.

Not long after that, the door of number 68 opened and two policemen came out with a woman who Tom assumed must be Ash's mother. She watched them go down the path, then turned and went back inside. He waited till the police car had driven off, and then he ran across the road and knocked on the door. She opened it and there was hope in her face, which turned to puzzlement when she saw Tom.

"Oh," she said, "I thought—"

"I'm Tom Healey," said Tom, in a rush. "I'm Ash's friend. I've come because..." Then he stopped, because he wasn't sure how to explain why he was there. But then she spoke eagerly.

"Do you know where he is? Have you seen him?"

"No," said Tom, "No. Isn't he here? I came to find him."

"No," she said. "He's not here. He's – well, I

suppose he's run away." She glanced up and down the street. "Come in," she said distractedly. She led him into the kitchen. He could hear Harry barking in the back garden. She sat down, her hands on the table, twisting a tissue into a ball and the straightening it out again.

"He's talked about you a lot," she said, glancing at him with a little smile. "And your sister. He was going to ask you round to tea, I think, but then ... you know about his father?" she asked suddenly.

"Yes," said Tom nervously. "He told me. Not much, but a bit."

"Yes. Well," said Ash's mum. "It's been difficult. For all of us. Ash was so excited. I think he thought we were all going to be a family and live happily ever after. But – there have been rows. Jack – Ash's father – never intended to stay here – he just had nowhere else to go. Then, yesterday he said he was leaving. He'd found somewhere to stay. I was glad, but Ash wasn't."

She had shredded the tissue into little bits. Tom remembered Ash pulling the petals off the daisies.

"Ash was furious. He went upstairs and slammed his door, and he wouldn't come out, even when Jack left. And then this morning, when I went in to wake him up, he wasn't in bed. His uniform was still there, so I knew he hadn't gone to school.

"I didn't know what to do. But I was afraid for

him. He was in such a state. So I rang the police to report him missing." She raised her eyes to Tom. "Do you have any idea where he might be?"

Tom shook his head helplessly. "No. No, I don't. I'm sorry."

Hope faded from her eyes. Then she seemed to have remembered something. "Just come and see this," she said. "I don't understand it, but perhaps it'll mean something to you. Come up to his room."

He followed her up the stairs and into Ash's room. Scattered all over the floor were torn up bits of paper. Tom picked some of them up. Most of them were so small he couldn't tell what they had been, but some he recognized, because they were like Sophie's card. They were parts of drawings of the Willow Man. He smoothed some out and gazed at them.

"Yes," he said slowly, "it does mean something."

Mrs Fox stared at him. "If you find him..."

"I will find him. And I'll bring him back."

He didn't know where Ash was. But he knew where to start looking. He ran downstairs and out of Ash's house, then cut through the estate and made his way to the Willow Man's field.

No one was there. No fire engines, no police cars, no Ash. Just a metal skeleton, a charred patch of grass and a few bits of wood ash which drifted lazily up into the air as he set his feet down. He looked up at the tiny head.

"Ash didn't do this," he whispered. "He *couldn't* have – could he? But where is he? Why has he gone?"

He closed his eyes and tried to think. Thinking didn't seem to do much good, so he did the opposite. He let his mind go blank. Then he started to see pictures. First there was Ash helping Sophie out of her wheelchair. Then Sophie was holding a bunch of flowers up towards the Willow Man. And then there was a man with a small boy on his shoulders, gazing out over a dark blue sea with sparkles on it…

Was that it? Was that where he'd gone?

Over the Edge

Without thinking what he was doing, Tom went home. It was the way his feet were used to taking him when he'd been to see the Willow Man. Mum was in the kitchen. She stared at him in astonishment.

"What are you doing here? Why aren't you at school?"

"I've been to Ash's. He wasn't there. He's run away." There was a sound; Sophie was in the doorway. Mum turned to her quickly.

"Sophie? Why don't you go back to bed? You need to rest."

But Sophie walked over to the table and sat down. Her eyes were fixed on Tom and she was clearly waiting for him to go on. Mum looked from one of them to the other and then seemed to accept that all she could do was sit down too, and listen.

So Tom began to explain. Not everything – that would be too difficult, and wasn't necessary. But just enough.

When he'd run out of steam, Mum was silent for a minute. Then she said slowly, "You are saying that you think it might have been Ash who burnt down the Willow Man? Ash, your friend?"

Unwillingly, he nodded.

"No!" said Sophie. She looked perfectly calm, and perfectly certain. "No. He wouldn't. He didn't."

Mum looked back at Tom, who shrugged. Then she looked troubled. "And why do you think he might be at Brean Down? I think you've lost me there."

Tom groped for words. It didn't seem to come to much when he tried to explain. But he was certain he was right – he just knew he was.

"Before his dad came back, he had this – this memory. He told me about it when he knew his dad was coming home. He was so excited – it was all he could think about. It was the only thing he had of his dad – just this picture in his head of him, with Ash on his shoulders, high up on a cliff above the sea. And his mother was there too, and they were happy. The place was Brean Down, he was sure of it. We went there on a field trip once, and it made him remember – he told me. That's the only place I can think of where he might have gone. Sort of – to get back to how he wanted things to be." He looked at his mother, trying to will her to understand. He wished he could make her see Ash's face, how happy it had been when he knew his father was coming home and how empty it had been yesterday.

"He could have got there by bus, I suppose," said his mother thoughtfully. "He'd have to change a time or two, but he could have done it. His poor mum – she must be so worried." She seemed to make a decision. "All right. We'll go and look for him." She put her phone in her pocket. "I suppose I ought to ring school, but I'm really not sure what I'd say. So I won't. I'll just get some coats."

Tom looked across at Sophie. She smiled at him. Her smile was growing less lopsided, he noticed. It was beginning to light up both sides of her face again, not just the one.

"It'll be all right," she said slowly, carefully. "You can find him. You *will* find him."

He hoped so. He really did hope so.

To reach the coast, they had to drive for what seemed like miles along winding lanes between low lying, windswept fields, till they came at last to Brean. The road ran parallel to the sea between plantations of white caravans. They came to a car park and Tom and his mother got out. They could hardly stand up: the wind was so fierce that it whipped their words away.

"You'll have to go by yourself!" Mum shouted. "I'll stay with Sophie." She pointed at the flight of steps that climbed up the hill. He nodded. Sophie couldn't possibly manage them.

He put his hood up and zipped up his fleece. He remembered the way from before. The path led past a café to the bottom of the steps. There were railings to hold on to, and passing places where you could wedge yourself in if you met someone coming down. The wind was astonishingly powerful, tugging and plucking at his clothes. Sometimes he had to hold on to the rail just to keep upright. He met a couple with a little child on their way down; the man held the child close to him, sheltered inside his coat. The woman said breathlessly, "You've a job to stand up on top!"

As he reached for the last bit of railing, he couldn't see what he was going to step onto. It looked as if he would be stepping into the sky. It was a strange feeling. He couldn't remember ever stepping into the unknown before. He took a deep breath and hauled himself up.

The path was very obvious and easy to follow. It was a broad swathe of cropped, velvety grass.

154

Small fronds of tightly curled, pale green bracken were starting to unfold on either side; he remembered that it was spring, even if it didn't feel much like it. A few yards to the left, the down sloped away sharply. The sea churned restlessly below, the colour of soft toffee whipped into swirls and peaks, laced with creamy froth. A couple of seagulls swirled above him – even they seemed unable to make headway in the teeth of the wind.

Tom set off. He put his hood up but it didn't stay that way; the wind snatched it off almost straight away. He noticed a sign. It said:

A NUMBER OF DOGS
HAVE BEEN LOST
OVER THE EDGE.
KEEP YOURS ON A LEAD!

He glanced nervously in that direction, conscious of a sinking feeling low down in his stomach. He kept well away from the edge.

After walking for about ten minutes, it looked as if the land came to an end a few hundred yards ahead. He felt puzzled. As he remembered it from the geography trip, the path had been much longer than this. And there had been a fort at the end – Ash had mentioned that too.

But it was all right because as he neared what looked like the end, he saw that, actually, it wasn't the end at all. The spur curved round and the land dipped sharply. To the right, and down below, he caught sight of a grim looking building overlooking the sea. That must be the fort. He plunged down the slope towards it and immediately the wind dropped. Relieved, he stopped for a moment to catch his breath and have a look.

The sea swept round the spur of land and then spread out to form a huge bay on the left. On the far side he could see the pier and the hotels at Weston super Mare, and behind the town the long crumpled fold of the Mendip hills. The down was almost bare where he was standing, with just a few stunted thorn trees, which looked as if an angry giant had tried to smash them flat.

Tom went down towards the fort. It was a group of grey rectangular buildings, some made out of stone and some of concrete. There were signs explaining the history of it, but he ignored them.

He went round the buildings, thinking that per-haps Ash might be camping out in one. But the doors were locked, and there were iron grilles blocking off archways and entrances. He called out, but no one answered. He stood in the middle of the fort, wondering what to do next. It was a dreary, bleak place. He remembered from the geography trip that it had been built originally to protect the coast against Napoleon, and then it had been used again in the second world war. People had lived there – even families. He shivered. He didn't envy them.

He'd been so sure that this was where Ash would come. But what if he'd got it wrong? He had to find him. He had to persuade Ash to come back. Ash mustn't be alone – whatever had happened, however bad it was, there had to be a way to sort things out.

He wandered over to the railing at the edge of the fort. And then he saw that the down had played the same trick again: even this wasn't the end. There were some steps – more of a ladder, really – cut into the cliff where it fell steeply downwards. They led to a grassy ledge, and from there a tumble of rocks fell to the sea.

Tom stared. The sea was a horribly long way down below, churning and crashing furiously against the rocks, sucking back and then hurling itself forward again fiercely, so that foam was tossed high into the air and then scattered back onto the surface like a torn lace veil.

An uncomfortable feeling uncurled from somewhere deep in his body and then stretched all the way up to fill his throat. He had an urge to step backwards, to find something firm and solid to press himself against, or to crouch down, to curl up in a ball on the ground. Anything to keep himself safe and away from that drop. He began to edge back, and then suddenly he caught a glimpse of something on the grassy ledge.

"Oh, no," he muttered. "Oh, please no. Not down there."

It was Ash. It could only be Ash. Holding carefully onto the railing, Tom called out to him, but the wind tore his voice away. Tom imagined his feeble cry swirling around, high up in the air, and eventually drifting down to startle a grazing sheep somewhere inland. He would have imagined anything rather than face up to what he knew he would have to do next.

If he wanted to talk to Ash, he would have to go down there. He peered over again. Ash was just sitting there on the ledge, gazing out to sea. Who could tell what was going through his mind? If he *had* set fire to the Willow Man out of an urge to lash out, to hit back at something, perhaps by now he would have realized what he'd done. Perhaps he was afraid, afraid of what might happen to him, of the trouble he'd get into.

Tom gulped. Why was Ash so near the edge? Surely he couldn't be thinking of jumping?

Tom looked round desperately, wishing he wasn't so horribly alone, that there was someone else who could go down there instead of him.

But there wasn't. There was just him. If he didn't go down and talk to Ash, no one else would.

He swung himself over the edge, with his back to the sea. He was trembling, shaking with terror. It didn't help at all that he knew most people wouldn't have thought twice about shinning down the ladder. He clung on, flattening himself against the side of the hill, terrified that the wind would casually pluck him off. He shut his eyes.

And then something happened. Suddenly, he couldn't hear or feel the wind any more. He felt safe, encircled by something huge. He could feel the touch of the sun on the back of his neck, and he caught a scent, not of salt, but of grass and flowers. His eyes were still closed, but the darkness rippled, as if he were looking up at the sun through a curtain of leaves.

His arms and legs had stopped shaking. He felt calm and in control. He opened his eyes. The wind had dropped, and the sun had indeed come out. He climbed down the ladder, his steps careful but certain.

Ash hadn't heard him. Tom didn't want to make him jump. He called, softly. Now that the wind had gone, the sound carried, and Ash turned. His eyes widened in surprise.

"It's me," said Tom. "It's only me."

"What on earth are you doing here?" asked Ash.

"Looking for you," said Tom, thinking that surely it should be obvious. "People are worried. Your mum. My mum. Sophie."

Ash looked tired and miserable. He seemed to find it hard to understand what Tom was saying.

"Why?" he said. "Why are they worried about *me*?"

Tom began to feel a bit desperate. He'd done what he meant to do – he'd found Ash. But he wasn't any too sure what came next.

"Well," he said, "there was the fire. And then – and then you ran away. So I thought that – I thought that maybe it was you who –" He paused miserably.

"Me who what?" Ash looked puzzled. Then, slowly, his face cleared. Then he frowned again. "You don't mean – you didn't think – you didn't think that it was *me* who set that fire, did you?"

"Well –" Tom hesitated. Had he been very, very stupid? He tried to explain, groping for words. "It just seemed to fit."

"Fit? How?"

"You seemed so angry. And you tore up all your pictures. Your mum showed me." He paused. "I thought maybe you were trying to get your own back – sort of lashing out."

Ash looked out towards the sea. He lifted his face and let the air stroke it.

"Oh, no," he said quietly. "You got that wrong. It wasn't me. I just needed to get away. I needed space, and I thought of here. I thought maybe I could get back that feeling that I had, that time I told you about. Of being safe and – kind of happy." He paused. "Dad left last night. Or maybe you know that, if you've seen Mum?"

Tom nodded.

"I knew, really, he was never going to stay," Ash continued, "and I don't know why it felt as if it mattered so much. It never seemed before as if there was anything missing. Things were going all right – more than all right." He looked shyly at Tom. "There was you and Sophie, and I felt – useful. As if I could make things happen, make things change. And they were changing for me, too – like at school, and the reading and everything. But then Dad coming home, that was like – like a dream come true. I knew that, more than anything, I wanted us all to be together.

"But it didn't turn out like that. It all went wrong, and there was nothing I could do about it – nothing. And then he said he was going, because someone he'd met at the pub had said he could go and stay at his house, and he thought it was for the best. I thought, what best? Whose best? I felt –

black, inside." He looked at Tom. "Does that make sense?"

Tom nodded, and Ash went on. He had never talked this much before: he was saying things that he hadn't even clearly known he'd been thinking. He didn't look at Tom as he spoke; he looked out across the sea.

"I could have – I don't know what I could have done. I couldn't sleep, and then later last night I heard the fire engines. I looked out and saw the glow in the sky, and I just knew what it was. Mum and Matthew were asleep, and I crept out. I took Harry with me so he wouldn't bark and wake them up, and we ran through the streets towards the glow. And there he was. It looked as if he was writhing, twisting – as if he was in agony. I didn't go right up to the field – didn't seem any point once I'd seen what was happening. So I went back home. And then later, I remembered something."

"What?" said Tom as Ash fell silent. "What did you remember?"

"Earlier, when Dad's friend came to collect him, I watched out of the window. I saw the car. It was red, quite big. And then later, when I went out, I saw a red car going back towards town."

He turned to Tom. "What if it was him? What if it was Dad who started the fire?"

Tom stared at him. "But why should it be?"

"I took him there to see it, a few days ago. And he made some crack about how it'd make a good bonfire. He drinks – he probably drank a lot last night, after he'd gone. He – I wouldn't say goodbye. I said some bad stuff. Maybe he wanted to get his own back. Or maybe he just thought it would be a laugh."

Tom was appalled. "You don't really think that, do you? He wouldn't, surely?"

"I don't know," said Ash, shaking his head wearily. "After all, I didn't really know him that well, did I? I never got the chance. But I know this. If he did do it, it was my fault."

"*What?* How do you work that one out?"

"It was me who took him there, wasn't it? And there was something more than that." He hesitated. "We all believed in the Willow Man, didn't we? But then I stopped. I stopped believing. I tore the pictures up. I did it. It wasn't me with the match, but it was me who did it all the same."

Tom was silent. As he desperately tried to find the right words to say, he was distracted by something stuck in his hood, something which was scratching his neck. He reached up and fished it out. It was a twig. He was about to throw it away, and then he looked at it more closely.

"Look!" he said.

"What?" said Ash, staring at the twig and then

at Tom. "It's a twig. So what?"

"It's not just any twig," said Tom excitedly. "It's willow! Look at the leaves! The Willow Man isn't gone – he was here!"

Ash looked startled. "Did you bang your head on the way down or something?" he said sharply.

"No, no, honestly!" Tom tried to describe what had happened as he'd been climbing down the ladder: the sudden feeling of calm, the feeling of being kept safe. "I know it sounds weird – but look! You don't get willow up here, it doesn't grow! Something happened – it did, I know it did!" He took a deep breath, suddenly knowing what he needed to say. "It was burnt. But it can be made again. It can be woven again. Maybe even we can help somehow – and Sophie too."

Ash gazed at the willow, and then at Tom. He didn't look completely convinced.

Tom said gently, "The first thing is to go back. You do see that, don't you?"

Ash took the twig, and put it carefully in his pocket.

"All right," he said simply.

When they got to the top, they found a path along the Weston side of the hill. It was much more sheltered on this side of the down, and now that the sun was out the sea was scattered with sparkles of silver. On the other side of the bay, the beaches were touched with gold. Inland, the levels stretched deep into Somerset, divided by the long, straight rhynes which drained them. And beside the rhynes, willows grew, and their slender branches swept the surface of the water, and their pale green leaves glistened in the spring sun.

When they reached the car park, they saw that there was another car there besides Tom's mum's. It was red. Ash stopped dead and stared at it. Tom looked it him.

"What?"

"That car," said Ash tersely. "It's like the one that fetched Dad."

The door opened, and a man got out and walked quickly over to them. His eyes were Ash's eyes, Tom noted. He looked anxiously at Ash. He put out a hand, but Ash stepped back uncertainly.

"What are you doing here?" he said, bewildered. "I thought you'd gone."

By this time, Tom's mum was hurrying over to them. She hugged Ash and beamed at Tom.

"You found him! Oh, thank goodness!"

She glanced from Ash to his father. There was something between them which joined them together, yet at the same time was pushing them apart.

"I rang your mother," she explained to Ash. "I thought I should tell her what we were doing.

She'd already spoken to your father, to tell him that you were missing."

Jack carried on, his eyes not leaving his son's. "My mate let me borrow his car. I decided I'd best come over here while she stayed by the phone in case you needed to get in touch."

"I thought you'd gone," said Ash again.

"So I had," said Jack quietly. "But not for ever, and not far away. I won't be living with your mother, Ash. There's been too much water under the bridge for that. But that doesn't mean I can't try to be a father to you, and to Matthew, if he can ever let me. I might not be much of one, but what I can be I will be. I wanted to say that to you last night – but you weren't in a mood to listen. And I can't say I blame you. I haven't been much use so far, have I? I know that." There was a kind of appeal in his voice. Ash looked at him but didn't say anything.

Another car door opened and shut. Sophie was walking unevenly towards them. Relieved at the distraction, Ash went over to her. "Steady," he grinned. "It's still a bit breezy out here."

Sophie's eyes held his. "It's going to be all right. Isn't it?" she demanded.

He thought for a moment, and then turned to look at Jack. "I don't know yet," he said seriously. "But maybe."

Rebuilding

It was one Saturday some weeks later, and Ash had just arrived at the Healeys'.

"Come on," he said. "Let's get that wheelchair out. There's something I want to show you."

"Don't need that now," objected Sophie, "I can walk."

"It's too far," said Ash firmly. "You can walk when you get there."

She would probably have argued with Tom, but after a few token grumbles she gave in to Ash.

"Where are we going, anyway?" she asked.

"Wait and see," said Ash smugly.

It was soon obvious that they were heading in the direction of the Willow Man. Sophie sat up straight as she realized where they were going. "I don't want to see the Man," she said. "Not like he is now."

"He's changed," said Ash. "Wait till you see. I read about it in the paper," he added proudly.

Tom glanced at him. "Read what?" he said. "Wait!"

Tom gave up and concentrated on pushing Sophie. "You weigh a ton," he gasped. "You didn't use to be this hard to push."

Ash elbowed him aside. "No stamina, that's your trouble. Here, let a man do it." Tom dropped back a bit, relaxing into the sunshine. He broke off a stem of grass and chewed it, enjoying the sweetness of the sap.

None of them had been back to see the Willow Man field since that day several months before at Brean Down – at least, he and Sophie definitely hadn't, and he didn't think Ash had been either. He hoped Ash knew what he was doing. Tom still felt sad and angry when he saw the metal skeleton in the distance, and he didn't think he'd ever forget Sophie's misery on the night of the fire.

The police still didn't know who had been responsible for the fire. They'd talked to Ash, but they'd quickly been satisfied that he'd had nothing to do with it. Tom supposed that whoever had managed to start the fire would have had traces of ash or even petrol on his clothes – it would have taken more than just a match, apparently.

Ash had asked his father outright what he'd been doing at the time of the fire. Jack said he'd been at his mate's house. Chris was someone he'd known years ago. He was married now, with a baby, and he and his wife, Deb, were glad of the chance to rent out their spare room and make a bit of extra money. Chris worked at the cellophane factory and was pretty sure that Jack would be able to get a job there too. It wouldn't be much, but it was a start. He'd been with Chris and Deb that night, settling in.

"Wasn't he upset?" asked Tom curiously. "I mean, that you thought he might have done it?"

"I was all right when you thought I might have done it, wasn't I?" pointed out Ash. "Anyway, no, he wasn't. He asked why I'd thought he'd do something like that. So I said I'd remembered that he talked about how it'd make a good bonfire. And *he* said that was just a stupid joke. He didn't mean anything by it, he just wanted to get a move on because it was nearly opening time."

Ash gazed very directly at Tom at that point. "And I believed him. I don't know if he'll still do stupid things. But if he does, I don't think they'll be that kind of stupid. And anyway," he added casually, "I checked out Chris's car. It wasn't the one I saw. The front was a different shape."

Tom blinked. The Willow Man was there against the skyline. But he looked different. The gaunt black outline was obscured behind silvery scaffolding.

169

"What are they doing?" he asked.

Sophie looked anxious. "Are they going to take him down?"

"Course not," said Ash cheerfully. "Just the opposite. Come on, let's go and see."

When they arrived at the fence, they could see a girl on the scaffolding, working on one of the figure's thighs.

"They're rebuilding it!" said Ash, a huge smile on his face. "They're making it all over again – he's going to come back!"

"Wow!" said Sophie, her face rapt. "Can we go closer? Can we watch her?"

Tom and Ash looked at each other doubtfully.

"Maybe not," said Tom regretfully. "Maybe we shouldn't while there's someone there."

They watched for a while, leaning on the fence. Then Tom straightened up. The girl had stopped what she was doing and was clambering down the scaffolding

"What's she doing?" he said.

"She's coming over here," said Ash nervously. "And she doesn't look happy. Perhaps we should go."

"Why should we?" said Tom. "We're not doing anything wrong."

"I dunno," muttered Ash. "They never found out who burnt it down, did they? She probably thinks we're criminals, returning to the scene of the crime. Look at her face!"

The girl came up to the fence. It was true, she did look fierce. "What do you want?" she demanded. "This is private property, you know."

"Please," said Sophie. "We won't do any harm." She pointed at the Willow Man. "We just wondered what you were doing." She paused, not sure how to explain why they cared. "We used to come and see him before," she went on. "It was awful when he burnt down. He was – he is – important. Special."

The girl looked doubtful. She glanced at the wheelchair. "Who does that belong to?" she asked.

"Me," said Sophie, glancing at it, "but I don't need it so much now. I couldn't walk, but I can now. I'm much better."

The girl nodded thoughtfully. Then she seemed to make her mind up. "It was me who made him," she said. "Then, as you said, someone – burnt him. That made me really sad. And angry," she added, "Very angry. But then – lots of other people were sad too. And I realized that the only thing to do was to start again, to bring him back. So that's what I'm doing."

Ash looked at her. She was older than she'd looked from a distance – not old like parents were old, but not really a girl either. You could tell from her skin that she spent a lot of time outside, and her eyes were like two pieces of sky. She seemed quite a small person to be building a giant. "You're not very big," he said doubtfully.

She smiled, and her eyes danced. "So? You don't have to be a giant to make one! You just have to start, and then you have to keep going. Come on over – I'll show you."

There were lots of bundles of thin, pliable lengths of willow lying at the bottom of the figure. She picked one up, and pulled out four or five pieces, trimming the ends off with a pair of secateurs.

"I'm Grace," she said. "Who are all of you?" They told her, and she said, "This is how you start." Her movements were swift and assured.

"It doesn't look as if you're making any difference, does it?" she said after a few minutes in which they watched, fascinated, as she wove the willow lengths together, making a net to capture a shape. "It looks as if you're just doing the same little thing, over and over again. But in the end, you can build whatever you want to – some thing small like this, that might become a goose or a dog that you could put in your garden, or something huge, like a giant."

Tom said slowly, "In assembly once, someone

said something like that. He said, 'The longest journey begins with just one step.' "

"Yes. That's it exactly. That's how it is."

She selected another length and threaded it through the ones that were already there.

"Will he be the same?" said Sophie suddenly.

"No. He won't be the same. But who knows – maybe he'll be even better." She paused. "You said he was special to you. Would you like to help make him again? You could do a bit of the weaving for me. Then there'd be a bit of you in him."

Sophie drew back, pulling her sleeve down over her right hand. "I can't," she said. "I can't."

Grace looked puzzled, so Tom explained. "She can't use her right hand," he said. "She had a stroke."

She looked surprised. "A stroke?" she said, "I thought only old people –"

It was what everyone said. "Usually. But not this time," said Tom. Grace reached out and touched Sophie on the arm.

"Maybe you could, all the same," she said gently. "If I start it off. Here – let's try. Let's just begin, and then see how we get on."

"Can I have a go too?" asked Ash when Sophie had done her bit. Grace looked at him. There was no nonsense about her, Tom thought. She had weighed them up and decided to trust them. If she hadn't, small as she was, they wouldn't have got anywhere near the Willow Man.

"Yes," she said. "Yes, in fact I think you should. And you," she said, nodding to Tom. "I think that would be fine. I think the giant would approve."

And so each of them had a little part in the weaving. Then Sophie told Grace about how they'd given flowers to the Willow Man and he'd taken them. She smiled and Tom wished Sophie hadn't said anything about that part.

When they'd all had their turn, Sophie asked if they would be able to come back another day. Grace looked thoughtful.

"Why don't you come back near the end? Then you can help me to finish him. Maybe you can think of something special you could weave in – a gift. Like you gave him before."

She pulled a phone out of her pocket. "What's your number?"

When she'd put it in, she smiled – a quick, bright smile that made her eyes dance, and then with a quick wave, she turned back to the scaffold.

And in only a few weeks, the Willow Man was back. Tom gazed at him from his window. It was odd, he thought: always before, the figure had looked sad, as if he was captive, as if he was straining to be free. But he didn't look that way now. He looked full of joy and energy, as if he was on the point of leaping off into a future which was unknown but full of exciting possibilities.

"Are you coming, or what?" shouted Ash from downstairs.

Tom closed the door and went down. Sophie and Ash were standing outside beside the wheelchair.

"Aren't you getting in?" asked Tom.

"No," said Sophie, "I'm walking. Because look!"

Triumphantly, she spun the wheelchair round. It was heaped with flowers – creamy ones like lace, shiny golden buttercups, long stemmed white daisies and scarlet poppies with papery petals and sooty stamens.

"We picked most of them from beside the lane," she said proudly, "and Ash found the poppies in a field. Aren't they brilliant?"

Tom nodded. "They are," he said thoughtfully, "but there's just one more thing. Won't be a minute."

There was a willow tree at the far side of the garden. Tom ran over and broke off a twig from it. He admired its slender, pale green leaves as he placed it on top of the flowers. He looked at Ash.

"I'm just giving it back," he explained.

And the three of them walked off down the lane, to finish what they had begun.